EGOFRIENDLY DOT ORG

BY

Joanna Ross

Copyright 2005

II

Dear Su

Enjoy ————

Luv

Joanna Rey

At the end of the runway, magic takes over……..

IV

Contents

VI

CHAPTER 1
A Breath of Fresh Air

The sun like some giant golden orb hangs suspended radiating life amidst the azure-domed heavens. Below, the atmosphere ripples to the shrill cries of the winged doves awakening the dormant to the splendour of a new day.

Do you want that in English?

The sun is shining. The birds are squawking. Global warming is in full force. In fact, it's a smashing day to sit indoors, grab a can of something to drink from the fridge and gently slip into a coma in front of the telly.

Wrong!

It's Hitler's, that's my mum's, cue for me to be dumped out in the garden to *get some fresh air*.

'Out you go and stop drinking that fizzy stuff,' Hitler commands.

'Why do you buy it if I'm not supposed to drink it?' seems a reasonable question to me.

'It's no good for you,' is the lousy explanation.

'I'm thirsty.'

'There's plenty of water in the tap,' I am reliably informed. Now isn't that useful information?

'How come everything you like is bad for you?' I dare to ask.

'Stop asking questions. Outside!'

'Ladeez and Gentlemen here is the result of the *Great Good for You Versus the Very Bad for You Competition,*' I proclaim in a raised voice with the aid of my air microphone, 'and the winners are............

> School and Sprouts…The Champions
> Crisps and Cola……..Forget it!'

'Would you like a thick ear to go with that water?'

I am brought sharply back to Earth with Hitler's rhet….rheta…rheto question, you know one of those questions which doesn't expect a reply. Anyway, it's obvious that **she** certainly does **not** want me to answer back.

Now we've got quite a nice house. It's always being cleaned, painted and rearranged or something. Smells pretty fresh in here to me yet I've got to brave the outdoors to *get some fresh air!*

The Olds are a strange breed aren't they? I can only think that this *fresh air idea* must be a hereditary thing. I reckon that they are paying us back for all their suffering when they were young. But were they ever young? Perhaps they were born already old? Didn't they ever want to stay in their cave and play *hunt the dinosaur bones* or something?

But Hitler or *She Who Must Be Obeyed* or *She Who is Always Right* has spoken.

My father jokes that when he first met my mum, he thought she was *Miss Right* but it wasn't till after he had married her that he realised her second name was *Always*. He says that if I breathe a word of this story to another living soul, he will deny it. Chicken!

'Saturday's my Day of Rest,' I moan. I'm usually good for one moan.

'So go and rest outdoors,' replies O Sarcastic One.

'But I don't want to waste all those extra computer lessons I've had after school (bet you're jealous, eh?)' I protest to no avail.

We've got two computers but every time I sit down in front of one of them, I'm told to *turn that thing off*. I bet Bill Gates wasn't made to go out and *get some fresh air!* Now if it's homework time and I want to get *some fresh air*, I'm told to *go and study*. Can't win, can I? Just because my mum is a teacher we're expected not only to **do** our homework but even worse get it in **on time**. Now who actually **does** their homework yet alone gets it in on time?

'Go and read a book in the garden,' orders Hitler.

'I've read it,' I reply.

'We've got hundreds of books,' she reminds me casually pointing to the neat rows of alphabetically arranged books on the shelves completely obliterating one whole wall of my bedroom. 'Take another one,' she commands.

Now why couldn't I be dis....disl...disleg...., you know that problem when you can't read?

'I'll get burnt,' I try for the sympathy vote.

Whereupon, a greasy plastic bottle is shoved into my hands which has an SPF factor so high that it's enough to turn the sun anaemic.

'I'll get bitten,' I plead.

I am instantly regretting that remark as she now subjects me to a savage attack of insect repellent. So violent is the Phantom Sprayer that within seconds there isn't a millimetre of my body that's not thoroughly soaked. I don't know what they put in that stuff but doesn't it pong? I understand why the insects buzz off; they don't want to be gassed to death!

So for the sake of world peace and to avoid being choked out of existence, I hurtle myself out into the garden through the French windows which, fortunately for me, are open at the time. To use the word *garden* to describe the jungle out there is really stretching artistic licence. Apart from the Oceans and the Brazilian rain forest, our garden remains one of the last great unexplored areas on Earth.

We have a garden full of plants which grow in spite of the Old Man's efforts. There is a gigantic holly bush which attacks you if you dare go anywhere within its vicinity. There are bluebells and daisies all over the place but I think these are technically called weeds. The green bit, which threads in and out between the plants or weeds, is laughingly referred to as *the lawn*. Clumps and tufts of grass are scattered about all over the place. When the Old Man pushes his vintage lawn mower up and down as he attempts to mow the area, he looks as if he is riding a bucking bronco. I'd love to challenge one of those TV programmes to perform a makeover on our garden but I reckon any decent gardener would get more pleasure and better results sticking pins in his eyelids.

I can state without fear of contradiction that we at number10 have the best display of weeds front and back of our house in the whole of Elm Street. Mind you, we lost all the trees during the outbreak of Dutch elm disease and nobody has bothered to replace them. I reckon they should shoot a sequel to the horror movie in our road and call it *Nightmare on Elm Street Because You Can't Find Any Elms*.

Inside the house is so spic and span that if you dropped a peanut on the floor, you'd fall over it. Yet outside is a complete wilderness. The reason is because *indoors* is **her** domain; *Outdoors* is **his**. **He** goes out to escape **her**. The official excuse is *gardening*; but *jungling* might be more accurate. Whatever it's called, it's definitely not very effective. You'd need a machete and a compass just to locate the garden shed. If you ever managed to get that far you'd probably find Dr Livingstone marooned in there. Something's taking its toll on the Old Man and it's certainly not the digging. He's beginning to look about 100 years old. Even the hair from his head has migrated to settle just above his top lip. She on the other hand looks like a typical teacher. She wears teachers' uniform; you know all sensible and boring, straight out of the museum and they even have the nerve to smirk at us saying that we wear a jeans and tee shirt *out of school* uniform!

Now, I digress; the question is what to do while I'm out exploring the jungle? I do not want to spend hours in the sun as I end up looking like a tin of corned beef without the tin! I know just the thing. This calls for an annoy the dog session. The dog is a lumbering great brute, black with white spots or white with black spots, I'm not sure which. *Damnation'* I call him. But you'd **never** guess what Mr & Mrs Nobrain call him? Yeah! Spot. Original, ennit? But with my red hair and freckles, I'm lucky to have been here before the dog and have got away with being called Sam. Otherwise, we might have been Spot 1 and Spot 2!

I think The Olds only got the dog because they can't produce a little brother or sister for me to beat up. When I ask them about it, they give me some old rubbish about some stork being too busy. You'd think at their age that they would know the *Facts of Life* wouldn't you? I mean they're getting on a bit, he's 35 and she's 33 but only admits to being 31. Dunno why. I told her the other day she looks her age. **BIG MISTAKE**! I'll be on bread and water for a month at least.

My best mate, Pete, is lucky. He's got a younger sister, Emily, to irritate. He can whip the arms and legs off her dollies quicker than blinking. When his Olds ask him about it, he says as bold as brass *it's nothing to do with me.*

Now if I try telling fibs like that I go even redder than normal. I look like a pumpkin that's ready for Halloween. I even manage the same stupid grin as *pumpkin head*; all teeth and blank stare!

I don't know who genetically downloaded this ruddy complexion onto me as both my folks have dark brown hair and the type of skin that tans real easy. It's strange, though, I do bear a striking resemblance to my dad's brother, Uncle Billy. He's decidedly got a touch of the carrot juice but then he's not generous with anything, let alone his genes. Even in conversation, he keeps his words to the absolute minimum. Apparently, he's currently *big in kangaroos* Down Under in Queensland. Where or who or what he was around 13 years ago, nobody seems to remember. Any type of subtle question from me brings on a sudden attack of memory loss to the Olds. If I try asking outright, I'm told I'm *too young to understand*; but on other occasions, I'm told I'm *old enough to know better*. Just can't seem to get it right, can I?

Anyway, back to more serious matters; annoying the dog.

'OK Dog, it's you and me against the world,' I tell Spot.

He barks but not in response to my challenge as his eyes are fixed firmly on the ball half hidden in my hand. He won't keep still long enough for me tie a piece of string on his tail. That keeps him amused for hours. Well, it keeps **him** occupied; keeps **me** amused for hours.

'You wanna play fetch?'

Spot barks.

'I'll take that as a yes.'

So I throw the ball into the undergrowth and Spot emerges plus ball. He drops the ball at my feet but I am reluctant to pick up the soggy sphere. But Spot barks and wags his tail enthusiastically so I repeat the process. He actually returns again complete with the ball half in and half out of his mouth. You may be wondering why there is an element of surprise in my tone. Well, to tell you the truth, Spot would be useless at mountain rescue because half the time he forgets to bring the quarry back. But here he is again complete with ball in his mouth, barking and dribbling simultaneously which is no mean feat when you think about it.

Soon it becomes a toss up between whether I get bored; Spot loses either the ball or the plot or the ball becomes too horribly soggy to handle.

So feeling like a break, I hurtle the ball deep into the bushes. Hopefully it'll take the dog at least an hour to suss it out. Meanwhile, I settle down on the only bit of exposed grass for a well-earned rest.

I just begin to drift off when the flipping dog starts yelping and whining.

'Be quiet, Spot,' I murmur in my semicomatose state.

This time he actually starts barking along with the yelping and the whining.

'Give it a rest, Spot, will you?' I implore the wretched animal.

The barking increases in volume. Usually by now, Spot's prey and his interest have vanished with equal speed.

'Spot if you don't belt up, I'll take you indoors,' I try the threatening tactics; not very convincing whilst lying motionless on the ground with your eyes shut.

Woof woof the deep doggy language has turned into *wurf wurf'* which has a hint of frustration in it.

I drag myself up onto my elbows and look over to where all the commotion is coming from to witness the back half of a full-grown dog protruding from a bush. Shovels of earth are being propelled backwards at great speed by Spot's front paws out through the arch of his back legs.

'Spot, stop being a pain. Come out of there,' I shout.

But the frantic digging continues. It's no use; I resign myself to the unavoidable fact that I've got to force myself up just when I am beginning to enjoy lying here doing nothing.

'What are you doing Spot?' I ask as if he is actually going to answer.

He completely ignores me and digs further into the undergrowth. As all I can see now of a once full-grown dog is a flapping tail, I decide it's time to go in. On all fours, I try to grab hold of Spot's collar whilst being showered with lumps of earth and dirt.

'Spot, you're not making this easy,' I adopt a musical tone.

Eventually, I get a grip on his collar but he pulls away from my hand. Getting angrier and dirtier by the minute, I reckon the time has come for one final lunge. My vision is now obscured by foliage and grit so I am, quite literally, groping in the dark. I attach my arms round the dog's middle and yank for all I am worth.

He's yelping.

I'm yelling.

I'm not sure who is making the bigger row as I haul him out of the bushes. I am tugging so hard that my feet start to slide forwards and I find myself falling backwards at a rate of knots stopping only when I collide with the ground coming up to meet me in the opposite direction. From my newly adopted horizontal position, I fight to stop the wretched animal from going straight back inside the bush. I've never known him this keen to retrieve anything.

I take a firm hold of his collar and try to calm him down, 'Quiet, Spot, leave the ball, I'll get it later.'

My words fall on stony ground. For no sooner have I taken my hands off his collar, than he is back in there again barking furiously.

'If you don't pack it up, Dog, I'm going to throttle you,' I warn as my patience is starting to wear very thin. But he is obsessed with something and is totally unaware of me.

'OK Spot, your time's up. You're going indoors,' I shout with murder on my mind as I reach inside the bush to grab hold of him once again. I'm struggling

with all my might but he just refuses to budge.
Something is sure gripping his curiosity.

'What *is* it Boy?' a question which falls on deaf,
floppy, doggy ears.

'Leave the poor dog alone,' orders a strange,
high-pitched voice from within the bush, 'and I'm
most certainly not an **it**.'

I blink.
Shake my head.
Yes, I'm still alive and not gone to heaven.
Must be the effect of the sun and far too much
physical exertion.

'Did you hear what I said?' there it goes again.

As to what it can be considering the circumstances,
my options are limited:

Option 1
Me? No, I think I would know.

Option 2
Mum on helium?
No, the voice would be right but the reality?
Impossible!

Option 3
The dog?
Unlikely, but at this moment in time I am prepared to
accept almost anything.

'Don't you speak when you are spoken to?'

The suspense is now killing me.

'I'm going in Spot, fetch,' I bravely declare. At which point, I dive headfirst into the undergrowth at the same moment as I hurtle the soggy ball as far away as possible for the dog to retrieve. Thankfully, the dog's attention is drawn towards the airborne missile.

Exposing my eyes relieved of all the muck, right under this bush I notice something silhouetted in the darkness by a shaft of sunlight beaming through the branches like a spotlight. At first, I reckon it must be a frog perched upon a large stone. But this theory soon bites the dust, when the Object proceeds to nag me about my treatment of the dog.

'Why don't you leave that poor dog alone and let him come and visit me?' demands the Object.

I am struck dumb which for me is a rarity.

'Don't just stand there with your mouth open,' **it** continues in a voice which is in charge yet not bossy, 'I asked you a question.'

'Please, let this be a dream,' I pray to the *God of Please Don't Let This Be Happening to Me.*

I usually pray to the *God of Passing Exams* so this is a bit of a diversion for me in the praying for help area.

'You're a bit lacking in conversation all of a sudden, aren't you?' **it** begins to taunt me, 'why not try hello?'

Words.
Thought.
Reason.
All desert me.
I am speechless.

'Well, really, a minute ago when I was trying to concentrate, you wouldn't keep quiet,' **it** sounds exasperated, 'now I can't get a word out of you. For a start, what's your name?'

'Sssss…,' I hiss.

'What are you some kind of snake or something? No, you're too stupid to be a reptile,' **it** answers its own question

'Who you calling *stupid*?' I'm angry now.

'Oh! So you can speak.'

'Sarcasm is the lowest from of wit,' I venture

'As if you'd recognise sarcasm even if it jumped up and bit you on the behind!'

'My name's Sam. What on earth are you called?' I'm not feeling too polite at this precise moment in time.

'If you must know, my name's Bud. Now if you would be so kind, make like a bumblebee and buzz off. I'm busy.'

'Waddyer mean, you're busy? You don't look busy to me. Busy doing what exactly?'

'As if it's any of your business, I'm emailing all the bulbs, tubers, and seeds under the ground informing them it's that time of year to make an appearance above ground,' Bud informs me.

'You're doing what to what?' I question more out of sheer disbelief than it being a genuine inquiry.

'Are you deaf as well as daft?'

'Now just a minute, I'm neither deaf nor daft but you're very rude,' I let Bud know in no uncertain terms.

I suddenly take stock of the situation. Here am I stood under a bush in the garden having an argument with what, at first, appears to be a frog on a stone. I move forward for a closer look. Bud is miniscule. His head is quite large and seemingly out of proportion to the rest of his body. His face looks all fresh and dewy. He is wide-awake like one of those annoying people who are bright and cheerful first thing in the morning. His body seems to be coated in a mixture of greeny brown suede. His teeth are white; his eyes are green. *His eyes are green*? Help please let me wake up soon! I'm giving *the God of Nightmares* a chance to weave his magic.

No magic wand.
Nothing happens.
I'm still here.

Then the old brain begins to kick in. As the blood rushes back to my head, a brainwave occurs; ET.

Bud must be some kind of alien.

'What... planet ...are...you ...from,' I decide to use Pidgin English.

'The...same...one... as... you... lot... unfortunately,' Bud mimics his complaint.

'Waddyer mean by that remark?' I stand insulted.

'Well if it wasn't for all you lot and the destruction you are wreaking on this Planet, we could be enjoying our retirement in peace. But as it is, we've been Noggin Napped for this job.'

'Noggin Napped?' I query in surprise.

'I don't know what you call this but we have been specially selected from hundreds of others for our unique skills to deal with this problem.'

'Oh, we call this headhunted,' I say

'Same meaning; different title.' Bud retorts indifferently.

'What do you mean **we**? You mean there are **more** of you?'

At this inconvenient point in time, Spot decides to make reappearance. To be perfectly honest, with the situation currently facing me, I had quite forgotten about the dog. He begins to make his presence felt by trying to push his nose under my arm whilst barking loudly. I am on all fours in the middle of the undergrowth having a *conversation* with *who knows what*. I just can't cope with a wet nose and more commotion to boot.

'Oh, go away, Spot,' I try elbowing the Brute out of the way, 'not now, Boy.'

I throw a stick which comes to hand. Fortunately, his low boredom level kicks in and he wanders off back to the house.

'There you go again taking out your anger on the poor dog,' interrupts Bud, 'he's only trying to help.'

'Now wait a minute. Wait a minute,' I try to get to grips with the situation because I fear that I am losing the plot at this moment in time, 'never mind the dog, how many more of you are there?'

'Oooh, hundreds by now, I should think.'

'Well, don't you know for sure?' I'm trying to get a fix on things here.

'No, I don't and it's not my job to find out,' Bud retorts somewhat angrily.

I can barely wait for him to finish, 'what do you mean you have to tell these plants when it's the right time to make an appearance. I thought they just popped up?'

'A lot you know,' Bud begins to sound irritated, 'imagine you are sleeping soundly under a couple of duvets, how do you know when it's daylight, warm and time to get up?'

'My mum wakes me up,' I reckon this is a dead witty reply.

OK, Smarty-pants, well there you are then, I'm kind of like your mother,' Bud's voice adopts a friendlier tone, 'think of me as doing Mother Nature's work. Several layers of soil have snugly covered these plants in the darkness for many months. When the climate starts to get warmer, we have to alert them or some come up too soon and get hit by the frost. Others like the rose can be a bit thorny at times. The rose, being the national emblem of England and all, thinks its blooms and aroma are far superior to some of the lesser more common varieties and so it likes to make more of an entrance later in the year. We manage to communicate with most of them in the spring but we never have enough time to contact them all,' Bud seems almost lost in thought for a brief moment but then pulls himself up sharp, 'now I really most go.'

'Just one more thing. You mentioned emailing, how exactly do you email?' I can't resist this question.

'We have a website, the same as everybody else,' Bud states the obvious, except it's not obvious to me.

'You have got to be kidding me?'

'Do I look like I am kidding? Believe me I would enjoy the experience but all the same I don't have time for that.'

I am beginning to detect a cynical side to Bud's character

'What's your address? Who set it up? I find myself answering my own questions, 'Oh No! Don't tell me?' I squirm.

'Yep, you got it in one; Spyda set up our web. Now I really have to fly,' and with that Bud vanishes.

Bud just ups and goes.
Don't know where.
Don't know how.

19

CHAPTER 2
No Show

Alert the Media. A miracle has happened. I'm washed; dressed; breakfasted and it's not even 8 o'clock in the morning. No, that's **not** the miracle. The miracle is it's Sunday, a non-school day and, even worse, it's half term!

If somebody had told me last Sunday that next week I would be up and ready before 8 am, I would have certified them as officially *off their trolley.* I did not get a wink of sleep last night and I am not normally even awake at this hour. But here I am, on the starting grid competing with the dog to be first through the French windows into the jungle as we wait anxiously for Hitler to undo the last of the Fort Knox locks.

'What's the hurry?' she asks with a sound of total bewilderment in her voice, 'yesterday, I needed dynamite to get you outdoors; today you can't wait?'

As the doors, heavily leant upon by us, fly open, Spot impersonating a large, ungainly greyhound makes a dash for *the* bush. I follow clumsily behind.

'Look at the beautiful cherry blossom petals resting like a beautiful pink blanket...........' mum's voice trails off. She realises that poetic observation is wasted on us two Speedy Gonzalez as we leave behind a flattened procession of pink foot and paw prints meandering across the patio. We are too preoccupied to notice anything picturesque. We are on a mission.

Spot literally nosedives under the bush. Inspector Bloodhound hastily begins sniffing around for clues. But soon the trail goes cold and the crazy dog starts shovelling great paw loads of earth in every direction with no apparent canine plan in mind but timed perfectly to coincide with my arrival under the bush.

'Cut that out, Spot,' I splutter wiping grit and leaves out of my mouth, 'let's try being a bit more scientific about this. Bud. Bud,' I call in a scouts' whisper in case Hitler is still earwigging from the house.

Despite all our attempts, Bud fails to show.

After two or three more hours of sniffing and digging (Spot) and calling out (yours truly), I reckon we are wasting our time. Boredom has set in.

Mother's cry of 'lunch is ready, come and get it,' offers a very welcome relief.

Frustration food we call it; it's one level up on comfort food. Instead of chomping away for the comfort factor, we stuff our faces out of sheer boredom and frustration.

Unusual for this time of year; unusual for any time of the year in this country, the weather is still fine and sunny so man and his intrepid dog, that's me and Dopey in case you are wondering, full up to the

eyebrows with fish fingers and doggy bites decide to
venture back out again and have another go.

By early evening, there is still no sign of Bud and I
have to admit, I am feeling quite disappointed. Never
mind there's always tomorrow.

The next day and the day after that are the same
performance. I am gradually running out of both
patience and half term. Spot has lost interest too,
though this is the longest spell of enthusiasm he has
ever sustained for anything in his entire doggy life.
But for the fact that Spot has been out there
behaving as stupidly as me for the past three days;
him digging vast potholes in the garden and me
talking to myself, I would swear that I had imagined
the whole thing.

Besides, Hitler is becoming suspicious of our
motives, 'what are you two doing out there all this
time?'

Then she ruins the mood entirely by reminding me
that I have exams at school immediately after the
half term for which there are masses of revision to
plough through.

I mope indoors but can't even concentrate on my
iPod which is specifically designed to take my mind
off both Bud and the revision. With my gangly arms
and legs sprawled all over the sofa, Mother says I
look like some demented octopus. She does have a
very warped sense of humour, you comprendo my

muchachos? How can I possibly relax with one eye focused on the telly and the other trained on the garden? I shift from one unnatural and uncomfortable position to another. I even contemplate tormenting the dog but my mind's just not on it.

Oh dear! This just is not working; I am busting to share my news with somebody. I am surprised that I have kept it to myself for this long. I can't mention it to the Olds for fear they will have me forcibly dragged away by men in white coats. Most of my friends possess the imagination and attention span of a goldfish so they're off the menu. The question is do I dare tell Pete and risk him blabbing it all over the neighbourhood? But if you can't trust your best mate who can you trust? I could let him in on the secret and tell him I would have to kill him immediately afterwards? But I've just got to tell somebody or I really will go crazy!

Here I go. I'm dialling Pete's mobile. Oh, typical! It's on voice mail so that settles that then I'll have to suffer in silence. Hang on, now my phone's ringing and it's Pete's number. Do I answer or not? Quick it's make your mind up time.

Oh well, here goes, 'Hiya! You busy? Do you wanna come over for a while?'

Pete's on his way over. He's cycling here and he just lives two roads away so I've not much time to decide whether to tell him or not. Pete's nearly a year older than me as his birthday is in September at the beginning of the school year and he's predicted straight A's in his exams so he's like got to be that much wiser than me, right?

I hurtle down the drive to accost him at the front gate even before he has time to get off his bike.

Shall I? Shan't I? I even now doubt the wisdom of my action but I do have to tell somebody. Pete's the ideal candidate to talk to. His name is Pete Cooper so I joke that I have my human PC permanently on hand. After all is said and done, he is my best friend and what are friends for, if not to give you undying and unquestioning support?

'You are, of course, joking?' Pete greets my news with total disbelief though I can't say that I blame him.

I think I should perhaps have let him dismount before I told him as his mountain bike is now on the ground wrapped around his ankles.

'Look if you mention a word of this to a soul, you're dead meat,' I cheerfully threaten him.

'Yeah! Yeah! Whatever! I heard you but can I just run it by you one more time?' Pete asks, 'you saw *something* sitting under a bush in your garden and you have no idea *what* it is but its name is *Bud*? Am I correct so far? You and the dog have spent the past three days looking and calling out for *this thing*? Stop me if I've missed something, won't you?'

'That's about the size of the matter, waddya think?'

'Well, with a lot of rest and time off for good behaviour, you should be out in 10 years or so,' Pete volunteers.

'So you don't believe me then?' I offer.

'Thousands wouldn't and I'm one of 'em. You have to admit, it's not got a lot going for it in the realms of credibility, has it?' Pete suggests.

'Well, at least, you're not laughing, I suppose.'

'No, I'm too stumped to laugh or believe me I would be rolling about,' explains Pete, 'It only goes to show that you are not completely stupid you just obviously have bits missing!'

'Why don't you come tomorrow and with a bit of luck if it's not raining you can see for yourself?' I propose as some sort of solution.

'OK you're on,' Pete agrees doubtfully.

CHAPTER 3
The Whole Bang Shoot

True to form; the following day it comes down cats and dogs the whole day. We spend hours on end productively staring out of and steaming up the windows as if by staring long enough we can will the rain to stop. The rain typically fails to oblige so instead we scribble in the condensation doing our level best to give Barry and Sue in our class their fifteen minutes of fame. Our artistic efforts are sadly cut short by Hitler's rumblings from the doorway to the lounge about *you should try cleaning the windows sometime!* She then decides she has had enough and sends Pete packing off back to his house but not before we have made a pact to try once again on Friday.

Friday comes around along with Pete. Luckily the rain takes a break. So here we are having some barbecue flavoured crisps washed down with gulps of cola for our healthy breakfast before we begin our trek into the wide blue yonder.

'Right if nothing happens today,' Pete threatens, 'I'm letting everybody know at school that you're one microchip short of a computer.'

'If you so much as whisper a word of this, I'll tell your Olds about how your sister's teddy mysteriously found its way onto your garden pond,' I retort

We call a truce.

More bemused than ever at our sudden attack of *freshairitus,* Hitler slowly unlocks the doors without removing the distrustful *I'm watching you* stare from her face.

Pete and I decide to *play it cool* by not rushing straight out into the wilderness in the hope that Hitler will get on with the ironing or something and leave us alone. We casually sit down on the grass, such as it is, and make out like we are reading our exam notes. In point of fact, we have a couple of magazines concealed inside our folders but she is not to know that. After a while, she wanders off to take the dog to the vet for his flea jab. Only problem is, Spot knows what's coming and is using his evasive tactics to great advantage and to the immense annoyance of Hitler. Still it takes the heat off us for the time being.

When the coast is clear, we saunter up to *the* bush and nonchalantly try to glance underneath. We must look crazy taking it in turns to bob up and down shoving our heads into an overgrown bush!

After about an hour, this pastime begins to get not only boring but very tiring.

'Are you sure this is the right bush?' Pete questions loudly

'Of course, I'm sure, it's the only one you can get under in this garden,' I point out, 'and keep your voice down.'

'This is thirsty work,' Pete complains, 'can't we get a drink?'

'Yeah, might as well, nothing seems to be happening out here,' I agree.

Four fizzy drinks later, we reckon we must make an executive decision. Either we go back out again and keep on sticking our heads under one very soggy bush or we officially certify me as totally barmy!

Pete votes for the second option whilst I think we should give it one more go.

Unfortunately, just as we are on the point of making a decision, mother returns with one very distressed dog. No sooner has she undone his lead than he acts like a carpenter and makes a bolt for the door. Fortunately for him, the door is open and he quickly vanishes outside.

I suddenly notice that Spot has headed straight for *the* bush and is rapidly digging his way underneath.

Trying everso carefully not to alert Hitler's attention, I hint to Pete that it might be a good idea to go back out into the garden, 'fancy hanging around outside?'

With all the delicacy of a sledgehammer, Pete asks, 'what for?'

'So that we can play with Spot,' I motion my head and hand sideways towards the garden door.

'What's the matter with you? You got something in your eye?' He quizzes me.

I cover my face with my hands and sigh in despair. For a smarty pants, he can be so dumb at times.

Too late, just what I have been dreading, Hitler asks, 'what are you two up to?'

'N...n... n... nothing.' I stammer.

'Now don't you give me the *nothing* routine,' she accuses, 'why all of a sudden have you taken an interest in going outside. Normally I need a JCB to shift you out the door?'

'We thought we would go out and give Spot some exercise,' I proffer in explanation.

'Since when have you ever worried about the welfare of the dog?' O Suspicious One queries.

'Since like now,' I suggest.

'Oh well, I suppose you can't get into too much mischief in the garden,' it's the old rhetorical question angle but she warns, 'I'll be keeping my eye on you two.'

'So can we go?'

'OK but don't make too much noise,' she agrees begrudgingly.

All systems go, Pete and I make a beeline for the bush which Spot is doing his best to demolish.

'Go away, Spot,' I command in a loud whisper which he completely ignores.

'Will *The Thing* appear if the dog is around?' questions Pete.

Before I have chance to open my mouth in response, a tinny voice offers, 'well I did last time and kindly do not refer to me as *The Thing* I find it offensive.'

'I'm very sorry,' I hastily apologise.

'I should think so, too,' Bud accepts semi-graciously, 'and whilst you are about it why don't you introduce me to your friend who will start to catch flies if he leaves his mouth that wide open for much longer?'

'Bud, this is Pete; Pete, this is Bud.'

'Hello, Pete, pleased to make your acquaintance,' responds Bud politely.

Unfortunately, Pete appears to be suffering from an acute bout of lockjaw and is apparently unable to move his mouth.

'Well if your friend insists on standing there like a human black hole, we won't be able to make much progress, will we?' suggests Bud.

Pete remains there rooted to the spot. Meanwhile, the canine Spot is going berserk causing enough uproar to wake the dead or, much worse, alert Hitler to the goings on.

I quickly realise that both dog and friend are in need of mouth shutting.

'Spot, belt up! Pete, wake up!' I try to bring some sense of order to the chaos. At the same time as I place a firm grip over the dog's slavering jaws, I deliver an awakening thump on Pete's arm. Undertaken simultaneously, these are difficult tasks to accomplish but they seem to have the desired effect.

Dog stops barking; will do anything to avoid having his nose and jaw clamped again; he hates it; admits defeat and runs off to seek amusement elsewhere. Mate finally comes to his senses such as they are.

Eventually we overcome our struggle to keep the dog out and us in to get a closer look inside the bush. Now we both assume the gaping look. In the middle is Bud, the owner of the voice, surrounded by what appears to be hundreds of 'em.

Walt Disney would turn in his cryogenic grave if he copped a load of this lot. Standing to attention like a miners' choir about to burst into song, are countless little figures in all shapes, sizes, and (gulp!) colours; all at once seeming curiously similar yet oddly different. None of them appears to be very large; in fact, they are about the dog's height which could prove really awkward if Spot thinks he has competition.

Today there is just enough sun seeping through the undergrowth to shed light on the ensemble without blinding our view. We probably will not be allowed much opportunity to assess the scene so I am trying to take in as much as time, visibility and brain permit. From their immediate reactions, I sort of have the impression that they resent being part of this *line up*. Not one of then appears to be happy to be here but looks can be deceiving. You will appreciate, of course, that it is very difficult to make an accurate assessment of their feelings since no two of them have their features on the same part of their anatomy as another; heads, arms, eyes, legs, whatever, seem to be either randomly scattered higgledy - piggledy or omitted altogether. I will do my utmost to give a rational and accurate description of the vision now presented here before me, however, if at any stage, I lose consciousness I hope you will understand.

To help matters move along, Bud shuffles forward, waves a couple of his leaves in the general direction of the assembled throng and proudly announces, 'Welcome, please enter. May I introduce you to EGOFRIENDLY DOT ORG?'

Bud draws our attention to the one standing furthest away from us who is a jolly looking soul with a huge lunar eclipse smile beaming across a large, round, orangey – red head which makes up the entire body. The glowing head seems to be precariously perched on top of a pair of miniscule flat feet apparently without the aid of legs. As Bud reliably informs us that this is Orb, a name that seems to befit this sunny character, the grin spreads from ear to ear except that this character doesn't have any. Two black craters form the eye sockets which are almost totally concealed behind a pair of bulging red cheeks.

'Upon these round celestial shoulders rests the life of this entire planet,' adds Bud proudly, 'Orb regulates the rising and setting of the sun and the moon. Without her devotion to duty, the Earth would have no heat nor light nor tides for the seas. Besides we prefer that while one half of you lot are awake, the other half is asleep. We figure that you can do less damage to the planet whilst you sleep. You do understand, of course, that you may be harming the planet but Earth has evolved over millions of years and will continue to do so with or without your greenhouse gasses. The damage you are causing will destroy mankind; it is you that are heading for destruction.'

'**Her** devotion to duty?' Pete and I question, completely ignoring Bud's insults.

'Yes, **her** devotion to duty,' repeats Bud.

'But that means **she's** female?'

'Oh, full marks for observation,' Bud wallows in sarcasm, 'you, I believe, speak of the Man in the Moon?'

'Yeah, but it's not for real,' I insist.

'Be that as it may, if you can have a man for the moon, we can have a lady for the sun. Orb is a Star,' Bud states with a kind of aloof patience.

At this remark, the protruding cheeks visibly swell with pride and pressure from the ever widening half-moon beam or should that be half-sun? I could almost swear that Orb is blushing but it's really difficult to tell amidst the rest of the sunburn.

'Shall we move on?' asks Bud.

Upon which, Orb retreats one pace backwards to reveal a character strongly resembling a lollipop which is anchored at the base by four thin rubbery legs; one green, one white, one russet, and one yellow. It appears to be festooned with the colours of nature constantly changing like the seasons as they spiral horizontally down the whole length of, I suppose, its body.

Trust me, this is not easy.

'Please step forward so that we can see you more clearly, Zest,' Bud motions the creature into the limelight and adds, 'Zest brings the vitality and abundant colours into each new season.'

I'm a genius as if there was any doubt.

Zest no sooner lurches forward to accept the acknowledgement from his Leader than Bud points out Ice next to Zest but neither Pete nor I can make out anything despite straining our eyes. Suddenly out of the gloom, the only mobile icicle in circulation becomes visible from a sudden streak of sunlight. Ice we are informed monitors the changes in the Polar Regions which affect the whole global environment. It is his responsibility to check for any visible signs of contamination to the area or the wildlife; any rise or fall in sea levels; or any movement or melting of the ice. Ice obviously knows a thing or two about melting and is anxious not to remain in the heat for too long. So after a brief uncomfortable smile accompanied by a swift dripping wave, he makes a hasty retreat into the shadows from whence he came. Bud excuses Ice's sudden exit by explaining that although we all need a certain amount of sunlight to boost our body's requirement for Vitamin D, some of us need a little less exposure than others.

Next in line our eyes are drawn down to what looks as if somebody has plonked an oversized rumpled cotton wool ball on the ground and a very worried-looking cotton wool ball at that. As Bud announces Cirrus, a small face reveals itself from beneath the whitish-grey fibres, deliberately intent upon keeping a beady eye on the proceedings. The extent of the frown which almost unites the two whiskery eyebrows implies that this creature bears the troubles of the world on its shoulders. I guess it must have shoulders hidden in there somewhere.

'Please forgive Cirrus if he appears somewhat agitated but he's used to floating about freely in the atmosphere where he blends in like any other little rain cloud,' Bud advises us, 'he absolutely loathes confined spaces.'

Pete and I feel like endorsing his feelings as we continue to shift awkwardly about in an attempt to get the numbness out of our legs or catch a clearer glimpse of the assembled mob but think better of the idea due to the cramped conditions. Instead we venture to ask without offending anybody what precisely Cirrus does.

'Because of the nature of his solitary occupation, Cirrus tends to be a little shy in company so I will with his permission speak on his behalf,' Bud looks for Cirrus' approval before going on, 'life on Earth is supported by the atmosphere, solar energy and our planet's magnetic fields. The atmosphere absorbs the energy from the Sun, recycles water and other chemicals and works with the electrical and magnetic forces to provide and moderate the climate. The upper atmosphere, the stratosphere, has the Ozone Layer which protects the Earth from the harmful effects of ultra-violet radiation and the freezing void of space. In 1985, Cirrus discovered that above Antarctica there was a hole in the layer. Your scientists have been warning you about the use of chlorofluorocarbons in products that discharged them into the atmosphere.'

'We learnt about CFC's at school,' I blurt out.

'Both Cirrus and I are delighted to hear that,' admits Bud as he exchanges a gratifying smile with Cirrus.

Well I think he's smiling but it's difficult to detect in amongst all the fluff.

If the next one is not wearing a brown and yellow furry suit being vaguely reminiscent of a giant, oversized bee, then it has a serious bodily hair problem. Whatever it is, it sounds as if it is very bad tempered as it keeps quietly buzzing to itself. Between this one and the next in line appears to be dumped a rather large pile of seaweed. It is only when two webbed flippers shoot out of the pile to acknowledge its name do we realise that this is another one of them. Bud introduces these two as Buzz who is in command of over one million named species in the insect world and Triton who rules the sea and all the creatures of the deep.

Standing next to the seaweed is an angular stone-like object with one eye staring out from its middle which immediately puts you in mind of a Picasso sculpture. I must admit, it's the first time I have ever seen a stone statue wave back as Bud welcomes

GM apparently for the first time to the organisation.

'GM has recently been recruited as he has the expertise to oversee the increased use of genetically modified or so-called Frankenstein crops,' Bud tells us.

When GM warns us by speaking through his left ear that *Nature does not welcome interference*, he almost reduces us to total hysteria amidst an otherwise sombre occasion. It takes Pete and me a superhuman amount of effort to stifle a laugh.

'We are grateful for you joining us at such short notice,' Bud thanks GM and diffuses a tricky situation.

Our eyes are once again drawn downwards by Bud to a sandy-coloured pyramid which encloses a revolving head. This is Dune.

'Approximately one quarter of the land on Earth is threatened by desertification,' the head resounds from inside the pyramid, 'usually as a result of man-made activities and climate change. I can burrow beneath the sand and by revolving my head I can assess these arid environments without fear of sinking or being coated in sand.'

This whole scene is becoming more and more bizarre with every minute that passes so I hope you will appreciate that I am trying to keep sane as I relay events as they unfold here before my astounded eyes.

Close to Dune are two tall, human-looking individuals. When I say tall, I mean sort of reaching up to Spot's chin though not literally, merely to give an indication of size. When I also say human-looking you have to use a fair amount of creative imagination. Their well-built bodies appear to be carved out of granite and are sparsely covered with Roman togas so that they remind me of those Greek and Roman statues that you see in museums. I suddenly notice that one has tiny fluttering wings attached to its feet and shoulders, with slightly bigger versions sprouting out of the helmet that it is wearing. The other looks deep in thought as if pondering its next move. The first one we are told is Merc, which is short for Mercury, who is responsible for all the flying creatures such as birds and bats. The more thoughtful one is Rodie who is the thinker and forward planner for the Organisation.

From the expression presently transfixing Pete's dumbstruck face, I am guessing that he too is struggling to hold on to his sanity. For we find ourselves crouching beneath a clump of overgrown vegetation at the end of my garden; tackling polite communication with shrubs, cotton wool balls, seaweed, lumps of rock and mini Tombs of the Pharaohs. What's peculiar about that? We have long since drifted past the realms of fantasy; we are now transported into another dimension. We will be scarred for life.

Ever aware of the work that must be done, Bud ploughs on. You must close your eyes to picture the next one located to the left of the museum pieces which is a minimised version of a tree which I will call a treelet in much the same way as a little pig is called a piglet. At the top of its stem is one egg-shaped eye perched above an identical shaped mouth, neither of which can be detected unless they are open. The stem is loosely decorated with tiny branches and leaves which are cheerfully being waved as a smiling Forest is presented to us.

'Is that as in *Gump*,' I reckon that's quite witty myself.

'Regular little comedian aren't we,' snaps Bud hastily, 'Forest as his name would suggest has the huge task of taking care of all the forests and woodlands that oxygenate our planet.'

Near the end of the line waiting patiently is a statuesque creature as if sculpted in marble looking decidedly Oriental and so delicate as though it might break at the slightest knock. As Bud introduces Tenshi, the statue gently bows forward and an exquisite smile disturbs an otherwise flawless appearance.

'Tenshi is our pearl of the Orient; our expert in the mysteries and wonders of the East,' Bud seems to have come over in a warm glow as he speaks fondly of Miss Lotus Flower.

In strict contrast standing next in line is a scruffy looking individual, without doubt the shabbiest of the lot. Here loiters with intent a hefty – looking brute, that is if you can imagine *hefty* in miniature, sporting a red Scottish kilt and scarf belonging to the clan McWeirdo. A tam-o'-shanter completes the outfit precariously balanced on top of its mass of wiry red hair which rambles down the sides of its head to meet a huge bushy beard climbing upwards from its chin. Shifting about like a prize-fighter ready to take on all-comers is Wee Beastie the champion of the animal kingdom whose antics practically obscure another dishevelled one hidden behind. Our attention is drawn to this poor soul bearing all the trademark of somebody who has either held a naked flame too close to a gas pipe or has stuck a finger into the electric socket with a few bright fireworks let off in the mix for good measure. Bud requests the tiny explosion to stand forward and be identified.

'Bin is the bacteria whiz kid,' says Bud and Bin accepts the accolade in a very chirpy manner. He bounds out smiling and waving happy to become the centre of attention.

'Most of you think of bacteria as disease – causing organisms,' Bud tells us, 'but in fact, bacteria play a vital role in the global ecosystem. The ecosystem both on land and water depends heavily upon the activity of bacteria. The conversion of nutrients such as carbon, nitrogen, and sulphur is completed by their ceaseless labour. What Bin doesn't know about bacteria is not worth finding out.'

Bin so cheerfully accepts the praise and his moment of celebrity in the spotlight that he is in no hurry to rejoin the ranks. Without wishing to spoil Bin's obvious pleasure, Bud fixes him with a stare intended to remind them all that *there is no place for glory boys in the organisation*. With that he ushers Bin back into line before continuing with the introductions.

When Bud next presents Ecosid, we could perhaps be excused for thinking somebody had left behind a long camel coat supporting a small trilby hat but as the headgear is doffed and replaced at the speed of lightning, we realise that something is contained therein.

'Ecosid monitors any destruction wreaked by you lot on the natural environment so in order to remain anonymous, he chooses to work undercover.'

'Not so much *undercover* more *overcoat,*' I whisper a little light relief to Pete.

Casting me a scornful look, Bud chooses to ignore the remark. Not far off the ground, right next to Bud is a kind of squat croc with brownish-looking, thick, dry skin which makes the creature look positively ancient. Before we have time to fully take in this apparition, Bud points to this shrivelled one to his left, 'this is Reptile known affectionately to his friends as Rep.'

Rep is apparently a creature of few words as he acknowledges his introduction with a massive smile which obliterates his lips to display masses of long, white, pointed teeth

'Oh, so he's like your *company rep* yeah?' chimes in Pete.

'That's right,' comments Bud deliberately paying no attention whatsoever to the smug grin which is likely to adorn Pete's face for very much longer if the remark is given any credibility, 'his really has been one historic success story.'

'Like what?' I suddenly become really curious at a point when I sense that Bud is anxious to bring matters to a swift close.

'He goes back to Triassic times nearly 220 million years ago, you know? But I can't go into that now as they can't stick around for too long. By the way, Spyda sends his apologies for absence as he is tied up with the web.'

We can just about cope with Jurassic after the movie but not well up on Triassic.

The formal introductions have received varying responses from the assembled gathering, mark you this is not the *Oscars* as the whole ceremony is despatched at a rate of knots by Bud with an air of having better things to be getting on with.

'Ladies and Gentlemen, welcome to EGOFRIENDLY DOT ORG,' announces Bud with immense pride.

Before we have the opportunity to ask who, what, where or when, they all swiftly scatter leaving Pete and me utterly gobsmacked.

'Food's ready,' echoes from indoors bringing us sharply back to reality.
.
It's getting dark and since we are never late for our grub, I figure we had better hasten inside before Hitler comes to find out what's keeping us. As I use every bit of spare energy to get my legs to remember how to stand up having managed my exit out from under this vegetation, Pete grabs my top to stop me as he obviously wants to talk about what we have witnessed. Hitler's curiosity has by now drawn her to the French windows to find out the reason for the delay so I put my finger to my lips and motion him to keep quiet.

'Same time; same place tomorrow?' I whisper.

'Agreed,' Pete confirms as the penny finally drops.

CHAPTER 4
EGOFRIENDLY DOT ORG

'I'm working on a project at Sam's house. Is that OK?' Pete gets his Mum's agreement on his mobile to be at my place today straight after school.

'Right, let's go,' Pete insists.

'No, we can't just keep wandering outside, 'I restrain him by grabbing his sleeve, '*you know who* will become suspicious and might make us stay in. Let's go to my room, get out of our uniforms and pretend we're working on our project, then after a while we can come downstairs for another drink or something when the coast is clear.'

'I suppose you're right, 'he reluctantly agrees, 'but I'm dying to find out more about them aren't you?'

'Of course I am, Stupid,' I reassure him, 'but we have got to bide our time.'

While I commit my school uniform to my bedroom floor and bung on something else to wear, Pete flings on crumpled gear hauled out of his bag. Next we wander downstairs where we help ourselves to a couple of cans of drink and a packet of chocolate rolls from the fridge just to tide us over. Before we can sprint back upstairs unseen, Hitler orders, 'don't eat too many of those or you'll spoil your supper.'

'We won't but we're starving hungry and we can't work on empty stomachs,' trails behind us as we charge up the stairs.

As we might have a while to wait, we try focusing our attention on *What did we learn from our visit to Kew Gardens.* The blank document on the monitor remains as vacant as our minds as concentration eludes us. Time begins to drag when you're bored.

Luckily, we do not have to bide for very long. After about an hour, Hitler yells from downstairs, 'I won't be long I'm just going to get some bread. I'm taking the dog with me.'

Bingo! No Hitler. No dog. Now's our chance! We hurtle down the stairs three at a time; fly out the French windows and shoot across the patio. Finally, we jostle for space beneath the bush and believe me this is not easy as Pete is huge for his age and he's already had his nose broken twice playing for the school rugby team so he doesn't mind elbowing himself into pole position.

'I wondered how long it would take you to arrive,' Bud looks up from his comfortable perch on top of a small log. He is seated beneath a canopy of intertwined branches; each branch generously decorated with perfectly shaped leaves; every leaf in varying shades of mottled green lit by the shaft of sunlight creeping through the gaps in the bush. I can be positively poetic when I put my mind to it.

'Stand a little less between me and the sun.' Bud quotes

'Eh?' I intelligently utter.

'That's what Diogenes the Cynic said when he was asked what he wanted by the king, Alexander the Great,' Bud informs us.

'Which one was he, then?' I enquire.

'No!' Bud retorts angrily, 'he wasn't one of us. Oh! Never mind; don't they teach you anything at school?' Diogenes was an ancient Greek philosopher who rejected social conventions and lived the simple life. Over two and a half thousand years ago, he believed as we do that *"I am not an Athenian or a Greek but a citizen of the world."* This is the way you will have to think; you will have to put aside your differences and work together if mankind is to survive.'

'Enough with the brainstorming; what does EGOFRIENDLY DOT ORG stand for?' asks Pete impatiently.

'What do you all do exactly?' I want to know.

'Whoa, one at a time please,' requests Bud, 'right now are you paying attention?'

'Yeah, of course we are,' we assure him.

'EGOFRIENDLY DOT ORG is the domain name for our website,' Bud continues without moving a muscle. I guess he must have muscles or how else would he move?

'You actually have a website, then? How does it work? You haven't got any electricity or monitors or computers have you?' I probe

'I already told you that we have our own website which Spyda so brilliantly set up,' insists Bud.

Pete and I cast a glance at each other in sheer disbelief. At least we are both crazy together and they say there's safety in numbers, don't they?

'Yeah but you don't say what all this lot actually do?' questions Pete.

Bud continues, 'all *this lot* as you so tactfully phrase it used to be called ECOFRIENDLY but since your lot are so obsessed with yourselves, your material possessions and have apparently no concern for what you decimate in the process we decided to dedicate EGOFRIENDLY specifically to you.'

'Gee thanks,' I acknowledge

'Don't mention it.'

Pleasantries over, we want to get down to business.

'We have various effective means of contact,' Bud assures us, 'we don't need to rely on satellites and microchips to communicate with each other. We are Nature Spirits or, in other words, beings of pure energy that have been brought to life in a physical form to represent our particular function. However before I get into detail, perhaps I should try to tell you briefly what we all do and then explain how the system works?'

'Yeah, we'd be fascinated to find out,' chimes in Pete, 'I mean some of them are real weird – looking aren't they?'

'We do not consider ourselves to be in any way weird – looking. We *actually* physically resemble what we represent which is more than can be said for you lot,' interrupts Bud, 'as far as we are concerned, you're the weird – looking ones as you so politely put it. Apart from a few technical details, you all look practically the same. As soon as we meet one another, we know instantly what each other's role is in life.'

'Oh, I see, you don't need business cards and formal introductions,' I suddenly see the light.

'That's it exactly; we don't waste unnecessary time. We get on with the business in hand,' confirms Bud.

'How old are you?' queries Pete.

'I thought that it was not considered polite in your society to ask the age of somebody older than yourself?' Responds Bud casting a disapproving peep in Pete's direction.

'Well, *normally, yes…'* stutters Pete.

'Let me stop you there,' insists Bud, 'so if somebody is not according to you *normal* then bad manners are deemed to be alright, yes?'

'Well, no,' utters Pete.

'Why are you humans so obsessed with age?' asks Bud, 'you use age as a barometer for measuring competence or as a symbol of vanity. In your so called civilised society, a person is judged to be either *too old* or *not old enough* for a particular task or they look *young* or *old* for their calendar age. We don't assess ability according to the number of birthdays that have been calculated but rather on the enthusiasm, talent and experience of the individual. We prefer to treat wisdom as our benchmark.'

'But don't you have birthday parties and celebrate?' I want to know

'Why do you need birthdays to celebrate? Your dog doesn't know when it's his birthday but he enjoys each day anyway doesn't he? Unless he is unwell, he had great day yesterday and he'll enjoy today and tomorrow exactly the same,' Bud explains, 'in your social order, age is used as a barrier to determine when you can start something or when you have to finish it. For example, you have to start school at a certain age and leave at another fixed point in your life. Then you begin work only to be dumped on the scrap heap when others younger than yourself decide that you have become *too old or past your sell-by date.'* We on the other hand, know instinctively when to start and when we want to stop. Only your so-called intelligent species ridicule those you consider to be different or less bright or older than yourselves.'

'I think I see what you are getting at. We have to know how old we are only to be told what we are allowed to do.'

'Exactly,' establishes Bud and continues, 'I have heard you refer to your parents as *the olds,* why do you do that?'

'Well, because they're not our age, they don't understand where we are at,' I have a go at trying to help Bud understand.

'Do they want to know *where you are at?* They've been there before remember? In two words tell me what your parents mean to you.'

'In two words, wow, that's hard. Um... I suppose... they....' I stall for time to think, 'I guess they know how to *be happy.'* What a pathetic answer.

'Then they have found paradise? Don't knock it. You cannot measure happiness. Your parents just want what is best for you. But I suppose it would ruin your *street cred* if you owned up to actually liking your parents?'

'What do we call you?' Pete is inquisitive and obviously not in the mood for *The Olds Appreciation Society.*

'We do not like your politically correct term *vertically challenged* it sounds rather like somebody who is having problems up a ladder,' Bud states in no uncertain terms, 'please refer to us as the Micro Helpers.'

'Where do you live?' Pete wants to know more. Pete wants fact; he's not interested in theory.

'Here, there and everywhere,' Bud carries on as though he hasn't been interrupted, 'traditionally, we micro individuals have taken shelter wherever we can keep an eye on you without being noticed. Our unique appearance allows us to camouflage ourselves in our natural habitat. So far we have blended so perfectly into our backgrounds that we have never been discovered. As more and more of the natural environment is destroyed, the risk of our secrecy being exposed is disturbingly increased.

'Look we get enough lectures at school,' Pete objects.

'No don't, I think it's interesting,' I protest.

'This is all very fascinating,' Pete moans, 'but all this learning is making my brain hurt.'

'Therefore, I shall bother you no more.'

'No, listen,' Pete is in command, 'if your hideouts are disappearing as you say, then why haven't more people seen you guys?'

'Basically, most of you are just not observant or bothered or too busy watching the telly or riveted to the computer,' suggests Bud, 'besides we really do not want to be noticed. If you lot become aware of our mission you will only try to analyse or interpret or, at worst, try to stop it. You would hold enquiries and investigations but, luckily they never amount to very much. Still, we would have to have a more furtive and secretive approach to our activities that would tend to slow up our progress which could, in turn, be too late to save many endangered species.'

'Why were we able to find you?' I casually ask.

'Big M is powerful but kind and considerate just like your mothers. She felt that the time is right to give you a little friendly warning. If you still choose to ignore the alarm bells and continue to inflict your damage on the environment, you do not understand the seriousness of the situation. You will feel the full destructive force of Nature.'

'What if we tell our parents about you?' I tease him to change the subject as I find that really creepy.
'I am positive that they would not believe you for one instant, especially as we would make a point of not appearing,' Bud assures us and lightens the atmosphere.

'What do you eat?' Pete is not bothered with this explanation.

'We live on LO's.'

'Do what?'

'LO's,' Bud repeats, 'well, you said you wanted to know.'

'What on earth are elose?' I just got to know.

'Leftovers, of course. You could say that we are your waste disposal unit,' Bud states quite factually, 'your neighbour next door, on the right if you look from the back of your house must be the *Queen of the Take Outs.*'

'That's number 10. We're number 8,' I reveal with hand signals, 'you mean Mrs Weaver?'

'Oh, that's her name, is it,' Bud accepts but seems more interested in the house numbers,' what happened to number 9?'

'That's the house opposite,' I try to explain, 'this side of the road are the even numbers, you know 2,4,6,8 and the other side are the odd numbers 1, 3, 5, 7.'

'I'm with you,' Bud acknowledges, 'well, Mrs Weaver has pizza at least twice a week; burgers, fish and chips, Chinese meals, Indian curries, with a spattering quite literally, of Mexican tacos thrown in as often as her digestive system or waistline will allow. You people really are the throw away generation.'

'We call her the *ping chef* cos that's the noise her microwave makes when she's finished warming up the disposable trays,' I try bringing a little humour to the situation but to no effect.

'Perhaps you can answer something that really puzzles me?' I think a frown has made its way onto Bud's face but I can't be sure.

'Try me,' I challenge confidently.

'Why do you buy food only to throw it away?' Bud does appear puzzled, 'and very few of you even bother to recycle all the packages and wrapping.'

'Search me,' the confidence has vanished.

'Why do you manufacture goods with a built in obsolescence? Do you understand what I mean by this?' Bud continues his concerned questions.

'Sure,' jumps in Pete 'you mean things are built with a natural shelf life.' I always know that *straight A* Pete will have the answer.

'Couldn't have worded it better myself,' Bud applauds verbally. 'You even dump your old folks in homes when you consider that they are past their shelf life. We have come full circle; we are right back to your question of age. When you reckon that something or somebody has ceased to be of use, they are consigned to the scrap heap. Nature doesn't waste. Everything is recycled which leads to an imbalance when you disturb the environment. These GM crops that you are planting all over the place are going to wreak havoc, you mark my words.'

'Revision time,' Hitler's words are accompanied by the slobbering dog intent upon joining in with the action.

Completely ignoring this instruction plus dribbling dog at my peril, I ask Bud as I am curious to find out, 'why what do you mean by that?'

Anxious to carry on and unable to discourage the irritating attentions of our four-legged friend, I squeeze the dog around the nose and mouth which is enough motivation to send him whimpering away.

'Have you ever heard of Sitting Bull,' Bud questions, not put off by the doggy break.

'Wasn't he one of the Native American Indians,' I suggest.

'I am impressed,' smiles Bud and continues deep in concentration, 'he was Chief of the Dakota Sioux Tribe, to be exact, who over 100 years ago referred to nature as *Our Mother*. He taught that "*all of nature is awake and has a place in the sun*" since all Native American Indians believed that you should respect all things that are placed upon this earth whether it be people or plant. *"Only by honouring Mother Earth,"* he prophesied, *"will we avert disaster."*

'Now,' thunders angrily out through the doorway of the house putting an awkward end to this interesting conversation.

'Why does everything have to be *now* for you people?' Bud looks perplexed, 'what's the first thing you look at in the morning. I bet it's not the beautiful day or the birds and the bees, is it?'

'Whatever,' drifts out of my mouth.

'I guarantee it's the clock, 'Bud insists with some certainty, 'you people are governed by time. Away you go now. The rest will have to wait for another day,' and Bud bids us a hasty farewell.

CHAPTER 5
Exam Fever

This week of exams is excruciating agony. They are proving to be even more painful than usual. Not the actual papers; they're a complete blur; no change there then. Like normally I've done just enough swotting to scrape by but now I find I cannot recall even the little amount of information that I tried to programme into my brain.

I just can't concentrate on the subjects as my mind is elsewhere; in my garden under a certain bush to be precise. Every time I manage a hasty peek towards Pete, he seems to be in a similar trance. The time is dragging even more than usual for exam time. I can't even spare a thought for what the results will be like.

That's only Monday; maths and biology massacred. We've got another four days, history, geography, chemistry, physics, English, English literature, French and German plus the orals to survive yet. To make matters worse, as though they possibly had a chance of getting worse, Hitler has grounded me and made me a Pete-free zone.

Tuesday and Wednesday are unbearable. I do not know how I am going to endure Thursday and Friday. I think I am coming down with something; something very nasty which requires bed rest for at least two days. I don't believe Lassa fever will wash with Hitler as I haven't been in contact with anyone from Central West Africa infected with the disease. It's ideal though as according to the medical dictionary, Lassa fever requires complete bed rest and isolation. I need a condition a bit more common to the suburbs of London. How about measles? I've had measles. What about the Asian variety, we've got Harry Lee in our class, he's from Hong Kong? I'm going to have to be a bit creative here. I could try covering myself in squiggles using my fluorescent green highlighter pen convinced that these are the trade marks left on my body when I was kidnapped by aliens last night. I'll stay in bed and look pathetic, should be easy.

I can now hear Hitler's footsteps mounting the stairs so I am running out of options – fast. Shall I make like I have lost my memory? She might be old but she's not stupid.

'Aren't you dressed yet?' she is angry.

'No, I don't feel too well,' drifts out of my mouth in my best weak and feeble tone.

'What's wrong with you?' she demands thrusting the palm of her hand on my forehead, 'you certainly don't feel hot.'

'No, I ache all over. I've got a headache and I feel sick,' attempting to sound even more pathetic.

'Well you were alright last night watching the late night movie till all hours. It must have been the large pepperoni pizza and two bags of crisps you polished off after your supper that made you feel sick?'

She would remember that wouldn't she?

'I reckon you have an acute attack of examitis and if you do not have a miraculous cure in the next five minutes, you will be going to school in your pyjamas! Do I make myself clear?'

'Must be your healing hands, mother,' perhaps flattery might work.

I begin to make this amazing recovery and get ready in three minutes flat.

'Hurry up and I'll give you a lift or we are both going to be late. I hate being late,' she complains as if it is all my fault.

Crikey, I'm now here at school. She would choose today to drive like a Formula1 driver, wouldn't she?

The exam starts in ten minutes. Which one is it this morning?

'Is it geography this morning?' I ask Pete. He's sure to know.

'No, you dingbat, it's chemistry,' these are the words I am dreading; not dingbat but chemistry.

'Oh, no! It can't be. I haven't even looked at chemistry,' my face and heart sink in unison.

We are now being ushered into the exam room.

This is my seat.

I could attempt collapsing on the floor but the school nurse is on duty today and she won't sign you out sick even if you are on a slab in the mortuary.

I could pretend to cheat by looking round at the others. Then I would be banned from sitting the rest of the papers.

I am doomed.

Mr Wilson, the maths teacher, is invigilating the exam and he'd love to catch me cheating. He'd be sure to make an example of me in front of the whole school and the Head would expel me. My parents would murder me or worse, send me off to boarding school. I wonder if they have boarding schools in Siberia.

Nothing else for it; I'll have to go through with it. Surely, I must be able to remember **some** of my Bunsen burner disasters in the lab?

No! Can't recall a single one of the experiments or what the results were. I have never known two hours drag so much in all my life.

To add to the misery, there is the weather. I mean, typically during exam time it is hot and sunny outside. Why can't they schedule these agony sessions for the winter? The sky is almost completely clear blue as far as the eye can see, interrupted only by tiny wisps of cotton wool on the horizon mirroring the woolly emptiness of my mind down here on terra firma. As you know, I can be quite poetic at times.

The man on the telly last night with his maps and isobars threatened that it would be 23 degrees Celsius today. In old currency that is something Fahrenheit. He neglected to warn us about global warming exam temperatures. All I know is, it is hot and it is definitely Fahrenheit as you get more degrees and better value with your Fahrenheit. Meanwhile, you sit sweating in a sweaty room full of sweaty, scribbling bodies. Normally, gazing out of the exam room window with my thoughts drifting away into more pleasant experiences doesn't bother me; this week is different as I find my mind wandering to a certain sunny spot situated in my back garden. I am thinking about *the gang,* wondering what they are busy doing while we are enduring mental and physical torture in Cell Block E!

Why don't we have the exams during the winter term? For a start, the weather is lousier and the extra time would provide more opportunity for selection to schools and universities. Most places are dependent on the grades that are achieved and these would be made available earlier in the year. Makes sense to me and we could concentrate the spring and summer months on sport or other activities. Every day we read in the newspapers or see on the telly that most young people are overweight or physically unfit. This would solve the problem or give us more time for picnics.

I try bringing my thoughts and gaze indoors. I am just being careful not to be accused of cheating as my mind wanders around the room, when it hits me! The revolting colour of the walls distracts me. Who on earth painted these walls yellow and a hideous yellow at that? They must have bought a surplus lot from the council, left over from painting all those no parking lines on the roads. I am busy wrestling with this dilemma when I am rudely interrupted.

'Stop writing now,' Mr Wilson's words bring me back to earth again. I had stopped writing hours ago.

'I'm starving. I'm dying for lunch,' I sigh heavily as Pete and I stagger out of the exam room.

'Well, you'll have to die a bit longer,' Pete adds sympathetically, 'you've got French oral before you expire altogether.'

'You're kidding me,' I beg imploringly, 'please tell me you're joking.'

'Sorry, Buddy, no can do.'

Now I'm really sweating. I think I am beginning to froth at the mouth. I genuinely don't feel so good.

'Are you alwight, Sam?' Madame Challon is prompted to say before she begins my oral exam, 'you are looking vewy pale.'

I am almost floating on her French accent.

Now's my chance to escape, I am now going for the even more weak and feeble look. Madame Challon or the nurse? I think I'll take my chances with Madame at least she appears to be on my side. Nurse Carole, who strongly resents being dragged away from her office and cigarettes, will only commit you to the Sick Bay if she can't feel a pulse.

'No! Really I'm fine,' I rally dramatically but still try for the sympathy vote, 'I wasn't very well this morning, Madame, but I came to school as we have our exams.'

'Zat eez vewy thoughtful of you,' she comforts me, 'per'aps, we should 'ave your oral first and queekly, no?'

'No...er.... wee, Madame,' I weakly but hastily agree.

Madame is very sympathique as I stumble through *my favourite fings in zee whole of France.* The Tour Awful is in Paris. Not a lot of people know that!

'I do not know how I got through that,' I confide in Pete as we stuff our faces at lunch, 'how do you reckon you are doing?'

'I honestly don't know,' Pete admits, 'I can usually bluff my way through the exams but because of you and that shower under your rotten bush, I really can't concentrate. In the middle of an exam I find my thoughts drifting. I don't know how my folks are gonna react.'

'Oh! You'll pass. You always do.'

'I'm not so sure this time,' confesses Pete, 'one time during this morning's paper Mr Wilson catches me daydreaming and staring out of the window. He asked me what I was doing, almost accusing me of trying to look at Paul Delingpole's paper. As if I would look at Paul's answers he can't even spell his own name right. Anyway, I told Old Wilson that I was just concentrating on a particularly difficult question but I don't think I convinced him.'

'How do you think you got on in the French oral?' I need reassurance that somebody did as badly as I did.

'That was a *piece de gateau,*' Pete can be such a pain at times.

'Ha! Flippen ha!' is the response **that** remark deserves and gets from me.

'Do you think if we told our Olds about *you know who* they would understand why we have been distracted?' Pete asks in a more serious tone.

'I had the self same thought myself but it didn't last very long!' I confess.

'Trouble is if they do not believe us and we get lousy results, they will think that we are telling a huge whopper. Either way, mine will kill me slowly after torturing the truth out of me.'

'Perhaps we could persuade Bud and Co. to make a prearranged appearance in front of the Olds,' I suggest hopefully.

'Do you honestly believe that we can contrive to get my Olds and your Olds out into your garden and crawl under a bush together to witness the Seven Dwarfs minus Snow White?'

'Yeah, right!' I see his reason, 'well, it's French this afternoon; I'll just have to blag my way through. Perhaps Madam Challon will be understanding after my performance this morning?'

The French exam on Thursday turns out to be just as painful as English and English Literature are on Friday.

It is now the start of the weekend. The calm before the storm. We are still no closer to finding a solution to our problem. Now we just have precisely one week before the dreaded results start; seven whole days in which to conjure up some fantastic, yet believable, excuse for our poor efforts. If we can think of nothing suitable we have but a few more days left to live!

I know the very thing to take my minds off our imminent demise, slow meditation out in the garden. After being confined to an exam room for a whole week of our lifetime, what could be better for me than a spot of fresh air?

My backpack is willingly released from weary, sagging shoulders and slides easily to the floor with a mighty thump. I shed my uniform with great relief all over the place, grab some shorts, and flop on the bed. Any hope of exploring the undergrowth quickly vanishes as tiredness gets the better of me.

CHAPTER 6
The Company Rep

Saturday dawns and I am no longer in the Pete-free zone as the ban finished with the exams. I will only get up now if Pete is coming over otherwise I might face the exam inquisition from the Olds.

'U cum ova?' I text Pete in case the Olds can hear me on the mobile.
'C U in 5,' comes the reply.

So I sling the duvet off me and leap out of bed. Quick look out of the window to see what the weather is doing. Exams over, this is the signal for the sudden deterioration in the climate. It's a bit overcast but at least it's dry. We should be able to get a clear look if any of the gang deigns to make an appearance today. Jeans are here somewhere. Just seize a tee shirt in the nick of time as Pete rings the doorbell.

'Pete's here are you coming down?' yells Hitler.

'Yeah, just coming,' I call as I hurtle down the stairs three at a time. 'Hiya,' I greet Pete, 'want something to eat?'

'No, thanks, I've eaten already but you grab something if you want.'

I locate at high speed a packet of jaffa cakes in the fridge and a can of something to wash them down with.

'Let's go,' I motion Pete.

'Just a minute,' Hitler interrupts the momentum, 'what are you two doing with yourselves today?'

'We thought it would be nice to sit out in the garden as we have been cooped up all week doing exams,' I use my innocent voice

'I suppose you can't get into too much mischief out there,' Hitler states dubiously, 'would Peter like to stay for supper?'

'That's very kind of you, Mrs Martin but my parents are going out and I've got to look after Emily,' Pete declines.

'Perhaps another time then? 'Hitler suggests, 'say hello to your parents for me.'

'Will do,' mutters Pete as I forcibly drag him out into the garden.

'What did you do that for?' demands Pete as he rescues his arm out of my vice-like grasp, 'I like your mum.'

'Done. She's yours and I'll throw in the Old Man for your IPod,' I extend my hand to shake on the deal but Pete turns up his nose at my *offer of a lifetime*.

'If we don't get outside quickly, Hitler will soon find something else for us to do like occupying the dog or running errands down to the shops,' I offer as an excuse.

We escape but can see from the look on her face that Hitler is decidedly suspicious of our intrepid motives. We saunter up the garden out of harm's way.

'I thought you would never come,' drifts out of the bush.

We both hastily dive under the bush to seek the owner of the voice. There sits Bud calmly accompanied this time by the squashed, leathery one with the huge broad grin which reveals rows of massive white teeth.

'Rep has taken time out of his extremely busy schedule to talk to you two,' Bud chastises us before we can get a word in edgewise, 'the least you can do is make an appearance.'

'I wouldn't fancy his dentist's bill,' jokes Pete.

With a fixed stare of irritation from his two protruding bulbous eyes, Rep responds in a deep, gruff voice, 'when one tooth falls out another immediately grows in its place. Does that satisfy your curiosity?'

'Crikey,' mumbles Pete.

'We are very sorry we haven't been around,' I quickly interject, 'but we had our end of year exams at school all last week.'

'Oh, how did you get on?' Bud enquires with apparent interest.

'We don't find out for about a couple of weeks yet, thank goodness,' I respond

'Why *thank goodness* do you not expect good results?' Bud questions.

'We'll know our fate in two weeks from now,' moans Pete, 'but for now would you tell us about Rep?'

'Delighted,' beams Bud, 'Rep which is strictly short for reptile is responsible for the reptile kingdom but his realm is much broader. Many reptile species have survived since prehistoric times and their success is in no small means a credit to Rep here.' Bud turns smiling towards Rep who acknowledges with a dip of his large head in embarrassed humility.

'Well he didn't do much for the dinosaurs, did he?' Pete can be so sarcastic at times.

'Ah, yes, the dinosaurs, 'Bud continues on a serious yet reflective note, 'they were lumbering yet majestic great brutes but why don't I let Rep take over from here, it is his domain after all is said and done.'

Rep accepts graciously and beckons us over with his stubby, webbed arms, 'Come; sit down; make yourselves comfortable'

I must admit I'm relieved. If I had had to spend any longer bent double crouching under the bush, I would have to walk around permanently on all fours. Pete and I squeeze together amid the foliage which does not leave much room for the other two occupants as the Old Man had taken the opportunity during the exams to treat the garden to a bit of *jungling*. Why he has pruned the bush at this time of year is a mystery known only to those who have had their brains removed at birth. It was lucky that he chose exam week because at any other time there is a chance that either we or the gang could have been in our hideaway. How do you explain your way out of the fact that Pete and I are hiding under a bush which we just happen to be talking to? Now that would take some creative fibbing. Anyway, we attempt to sit down but are so cramped that this can hardly be described as comfortable or even sane for that matter.

Rep pinches the edges of his lapels between his webbed fingers as he adopts a pastoral pose and carries on unperturbed, 'now I want you to close your eyes and cast your minds back not thousands but millions of years, about 220 million give or take a few million way back to the Triassic period. It is called the "Age of Dinosaurs" and often referred to as the "Age of Reptiles." The world map at that time would not be recognisable as the world of today. The continents shifted so that they were no longer connected and formed their current outline. Are you with me so far,' he beams.

We are mesmerised but sit upright to demonstrate that we are an appreciative, if not, captive audience.

So, assured that we are with him every verbal step of the way, he dreamily casts those huge eyes upwards towards the heavens or to the top of the bush whichever grabs your imagination.

After a brief interval, he then proceeds, 'the first crocodile or *protosuchus* roamed the Earth about 240 million years ago which evolved nearly 150 million years ago into the familiar shape that you recognise today and the crocodilians remain the longest surviving species of any land animal on the planet. That's a long time when you think about it since human beings or *homo sapiens* have only been around for less than 200,000 years. We have managed to survive almost unchanged for the past 65 million years and are one of the few remaining relatives of the dinosaurs which ruled the world for over 160 million years, Dinosaurs were abundant and they consumed enough food per day to satisfy an army of locusts. So after about 160 million years of dinosaur domination, Big M came to the conclusion that they had to make way for more intelligent creatures if this planet was to develop. The dinosaurs had outlived their usefulness.' Rep stops for a while, his thoughts still deep in the past; his voice tinged with sadness.

Rep sighs.

Wish he hadn't.

Phew! Now we see why they keep needing new teeth if their breath is anything to go by.

Perhaps Pete and I could develop a green and white striped toothpaste especially for reptiles. Just imagine me and Pete on YouTube broadcasting "Reptident" or "Colgator" the toothpaste for "Snappy Happy Teeth." We could be millionaires.

My daydream bubble of fame and fortune is sharply burst by Bud who sensing Rep's emotion picks up the story while our walking, talking handbag composes himself, 'Ah, but just reflect upon your numerous successes.'

'You mean to say that Big M deliberately did away with the dinosaurs and who is Big M anyway?' Pete asks.

'Two questions in one go,' Bud comments, 'I'll see if I can reply as quickly. Yes, in order for this planet to progress the dinosaurs had to go.'

'That's sad,' I complain

'Progress is often cruel but sometimes necessary. However, there's progress and there's progress. I use the biological meaning of the word *progress,* which is *adaptation,* and not the more common meaning of *advancement*,' Bud explains, 'but whether the world is a better place with you lot instead of the dinosaurs is a matter for conjecture.'

'Who is this Big M?' Pete ignores the lecture.

'If you stop interrupting, I'll tell you. Big M is Mother Nature, Controller of everything natural.'

'I thought the dinosaurs were wiped out by an asteroid crashing onto the Earth,' I try to display my limited knowledge.

'Big M, or The Boss as we like to refer to her, realised that she would need something forceful and dramatic to eradicate those monster creations. So she arranged for a giant asteroid to collide with the Earth some 65 million years ago. The impact near the town of Chicxulub in Mexico formed a crater 38 km deep and 200 km wide.'

'How come that caused a mass extinction?'

'The explosion was equivalent to all the atomic weapons on the planet going off at once,' Rep has all the details, 'the fireball which followed the impact burnt most of the vegetation and devastated the landscape. The force also triggered a massive earthquake. Over 70% of all species were destroyed. Such was the environmental disaster it took over 15 million years afterwards for the planet and the surviving species to begin to recover.'

'How did you survive?' Pete takes the words right out of my mouth.

'Big M wanted you to have some examples of living prehistoric life. There are over 23 varieties of crocodilian species still roaming the Earth today.' Rep proudly announces.

'Why only you?' Pete is like a dog with a bone; he won't let go.

'We were not alone; there were many others which you no doubt have heard of such as snakes, lizards, sharks, turtles and tortoises?' Rep is pleased to tell us.

'How did you manage it?' I butt in; reckon it's my turn.

'Where do I begin?' ponders Rep,' for a start we have no natural enemies except Man and we scare most of them. We can stay under water for 6 hours or more by reducing our heart rate to 3 beats per minute so we need less oxygen to breath. So by staying submerged we were able to escape the fires that followed the impact and by keeping warm under water we could avoid the freezing temperatures which lasted for a number of years afterwards. We eat decaying meat as well as fresh and can last up to 3 years between meals. Whereas reptiles usually abandon their young, we protect ours. To survive; you have to adapt.'

'I know that there are millions of snakes and crocodiles all over the world now is that due to you?' I question, 'but what happened to the mammoth?'

If I could bottle pride, now would be my opportunity as Rep grins which is difficult with all those molars and takes a satisfied bow, 'I believe I can take the credit for the success of the snakes and the crocodiles but the mammoth was another sacrifice to progress.'

'You mean The Boss did away with the mammoths as well? What a ratbag.' Pete comments in disbelief.

'She is most certainly *not* a whatever you called Her. By the way, whenever you lot want to be insulting, why do you use a member of the animal kingdom in the title?' Rep has now lost his polite smile.

'What do you mean?' queries Pete.

'Well, the term *ratrace is* used by you to describe your continued routine of hectic competitive activities. Animals do not hurtle around in ever decreasing circles; chasing the clock; causing high blood pressure and rage attacks. Without the aid of watches or clocks, jellyfish, crabs, caribou and rats know exactly where to go and when. These animals sense the importance of time but they rely upon their body clocks which are far more reliable. They depend upon their internal clocks for their very survival and their ability to evolve into adapted versions of their species. Many of these have survived far longer than humans. Perhaps your dependence on your watches is slowing your evolution? Perhaps you are living on borrowed time?' Bud stops to give us time to think.

We both shift about uneasily and uncomfortably.

Bud decides the pause is long enough, 'As a matter of fact, some 70,000 years ago during the Stone Age, the human population had a brush with extinction; extreme environmental conditions reduced numbers down to about 2,000 in total. If the human race had then been hit with disease it could quite easily have vanished off the face of the earth. All that would have remained to prove you ever existed would have been your fossilised bones. If Big M suspects that you are not looking after the planet up to her expectations, she could just as easily ensure that you share the same fate as the dinosaurs.'

'You mean she could do away with us?' I ask hoping that he is not being serious, 'why would she want to?'

'Absolutely, she has organised your evolution through the ages by a process called natural selection but she could just as easily decide that you are past your sell-by date. She could induce another Ice Age or arrange for another collision course with a passing asteroid or take as another example the volcano in Yellowstone National Park in the States which is rumoured to be *the place where hell bubbles up* which has been on a regular eruption cycle of every 600,000 years. The last eruption was 640,000 years ago so the next is well overdue,' Bud alarmingly advises me.

'Crikey,' I spurt forth in disbelief, 'you mean she does this on purpose? She wouldn't would she?

'Depends how angry she is. You can tell the strength of her temper by the force of the typhoons, the monsoon rains, the earthquakes, the famines or the droughts,' Bud actually begins to frighten me, 'when you have wars amongst yourselves or acts of terrorism, she becomes really incensed at the sheer unnecessary waste of life and destruction of irreplaceable natural habitat.'

'Yeah but who would she replace us with,' I say quite confidently, 'there is no other species as intelligent as us?'

'Machines,' Bud says in a very matter-of-fact way.

'Machines?' I repeat in shock, 'how are machines cleverer than us?'

'How often do you trust your lives to machines?' he asks directly, 'in planes, cars or trains for example. You are enslaved to machines. Machines can fly or travel at high speeds; you can't. They can manufacture other machines; they can cook; they can generate extreme heat or cold and they can even clean.'

'Ah but they can't think or reason,' states Pete with an air of *get out of that one.*

'Oh no, what about computers and robots?' poses Bud, 'You could so easily be made redundant.'

'She does all this deliberately?' I change the subject before my back turns completely to jelly.

'For sure, she likes to let you know who's Boss.'

'Sounds like my mother,' I add in jest.

'In a similar sort of way just as your mother is responsible for the survival of your family, Big M has to ensure that that the Earth and the universe exist to be explored There are so many creations on this planet to wonder at and still so many more yet to be discovered. Then there is space and the multiverse,' Bud attempts to reassure me, 'anyway, back to the animals, why do you habitually refer to other members of your species as pig, dog or cow, for example, when you wish to offend somebody?'

'That has always puzzled me. Why is this?' Rep now joins in.

'I never really thought about it before,' Pete responds, 'but I guess we do have a habit of using animals names as a means of insult.'

'Is this because you regard animals as inferior to yourselves?' Bud interrupts in a sarcastic tone, 'If a cat falls from a height, it will land feet first; you will never find a butterfly out in the rain; penguins don't wear shoes but their feet don't stick to the ice. So what makes you think you are so smart?'

'Can't we get on before Sam's mother comes out to find us? Let's get back to the reptiles and the mammoth that's far more interesting. Besides I've got cramp in both my feet,' groans Pete shortly before he knees me in the back as he attempts to shift position in our confined situation.

Bud steps forth, 'we will have to leave that to another day when Wee Beastie can take the credit for the survival of the animal kingdom.'

'I get really upset when I hear facts about animals not surviving,' I express my genuine concern.

'Don't waste your time worrying **do** something about it,' Bud stresses, 'worrying is like sitting in a rocking chair; it keeps you occupied but gets you nowhere. This planet is our precious legacy. It has been entrusted to us and it is our duty to preserve it. Although the world today is full of technology, we are more animal than machine. We live in an artificial world but belong to the natural one. We identify more with Nature.'

ı nere is no answer to that. Just in the nick of time, Hitler's voice bellows from the kitchen, 'lunch is ready.'

'We'd better go or she will come looking for us,' I suggest. Besides as fascinated as I am, I could do with stretching my legs before rigor mortis sets in, 'could we possibly continue after we've eaten?'

'We could spare a little more time,' Bud's voice rises in expectation, 'if perhaps we could persuade you to smuggle out some leftovers for us?'

'No problem,' I state quite confidently as Pete and I stagger to once again stand up to our full height, 'we'll be about twenty minutes is that alright?'

'We'll be waiting for you.'

As we make our way to the house, the salivating whiff of hamburgers and chips wafts towards our lips. How are we going to hide hot chips and burgers without being seen?' Pete thinks out loud.

'Inspiration will come to me as we are eating,' I sound convincing, 'but lay off the tomato ketchup or everything will be too soggy.'

We sit at the kitchen table trying to delay the need to satisfy our overpowering hunger in the hope that Hitler might be distracted just long enough for us to slip some scraps into our pockets.

'I thought you two would be ravenous?' Hitler is suspicious, 'you've normally demolished your food by now.'

'We're just savouring our food, Mrs Martin,' says Pete very unconvincingly.

'That's very thoughtful of you, Peter,' replies Hitler even more unconvincingly. Pete smiles his *I hate being called Peter smile.* Luckily, she can't stand the spectacle of us munching so slowly and decides to go upstairs. We hastily grab some paper towel to wrap up the remains of our lunch.

'Thanks for lunch,' we call out as we head into the garden once again clutching our soggy parcels close to our bodies. We hurry back to the bush to find our two wee friends eagerly awaiting our return still perched upon a stone.

'You're here; that's good because we've managed to scrounge some food for you. We hope you like the remains of hamburgers and chips?' I say as we creep under the bush and cheerfully hand over our food offerings, 'thanks to Pete here, I hope your taste buds are tuned into tomato ketchup?'

'Sounds delicious,' replies Bud, 'and we are quite used to ketchup as we believe your neighbour three doors down even drowns his cornflakes in tomato sauce. Everything they throw away is virtually swimming in the stuff.'

They set about the nibbles as if they haven't eaten for a month. I wouldn't care to enter a food eating competition against these two. They must be the fastest noshers in the Western Hemisphere.

'That was superb. Thank you,' acknowledges Bud gratefully.

Not quite knowing what to say I suggest, 'perhaps we could bring you something to eat every day?'

'That's very thoughtful of you,' Bud responds with a huge smile on his face, 'but we can't guarantee to be here all the time and besides it might make your parents suspicious.'

'Will you be here tomorrow?' Pete is seriously interested I can tell by the tone of his voice.

'Doubtful, as we have spent today with you and we are behind with our duties but we will be back. Now we must take our leave of you,' Bud's little voice vanishes as quickly as he does.

'How do they do that,' wonders Pete, 'how do they disappear right in front of our eyes?'

'Got to be the speed with which they move, I guess,' I offer as we try to get up in slow motion.

'Shall I bowl round tomorrow?' enquires Pete.

'Yeah, if you like. After ten, I should be awake.'

CHAPTER 7
Buzzing Around

Sunday comes and goes quietly. Pete is collared into going out en famille to visit some ancient relatives. He asks me if I would like to go along but as tempting as the offer is I would rather drown myself.

I dash out into the garden and take a quick look under the bush but I am not surprised to find nobody there after our long session yesterday. It's back to school tomorrow and worse, results!!! Today I have to concentrate on finding a plausible excuse for my pathetic performance in the exams.

I wish Pete were around; he's good at producing believable excuses. Perhaps, I can conjure up one or two and then run them past him later today:

1. We were both abducted by aliens who used probes to blank out our minds for one week.
2. We fell off our bikes and hit our heads which caused exam amnesia.
3. The Head decided not to grade the papers this term.
4. The staff has gone on strike and refuse to mark the papers.
5. We communicated with some little creatures about the power of Nature under a bush in the garden and could not concentrate on our work.

I am spoilt for choice. Any medical reason will require a certificate from the doctor. I don't somehow believe my *conversations with Nature* will hold up in court. At this moment in time, I favour the one about the aliens. Whichever way I look at the problem, I am in **big** trouble. HELP!

I am dreading telling the Old Man that his Number One son is a failure. Sons of bank managers are not allowed the privilege of failing. I am not sure whether it is a requirement for all bank managers to be devoid of a sense of humour but my father cannot see the funny side of anything. Perhaps it is a condition of birth? However, since I was not around when he first made his appearance on this planet, I can neither confirm nor deny this fact. Only one thing is certain, my father must have fallen off the conveyor belt when the *Powers that Be* were doling out the gift of laughter. Though I would not imagine that spending all day counting other people's money would be a barrel of laughs.

Hitler on the other hand despite being a teacher is prone to the occasional moment of mirth. She does have one major fault that since she teaches English she expects me to be an A plus, plus, plus student in the wretched subject. Genius is definitely not hereditary; thank goodness neither is being miserable. Mind you, it will take the genius of Einstein to persuade these two that bombing out in every exam is in any way, shape, or form something to laugh about.

Pete has not called so I figure he has had no time to think of a logical reason either. I manage to make it to suppertime unscathed but without an excuse ready to hand. I will have to box clever for the time being.

'You haven't touched your supper,' Hitler remarks, 'what's wrong you seem all jittery?'

I have to confess my mind is elsewhere as I lamely answer, 'I've got a headache.'

'You spent too long out in the sun yesterday. I bet you didn't put on any sun lotion, did you?' she inquisitions me.

'No, that must be the reason. I think I'll have an early night,' I try to look poorly to avoid any suspicion.

'Night,' I feebly call as I stagger up to my room. I leap onto the bed and try to make contact with Pete. All to no avail as his phone is switched off. I daren't leave a message for fear of interception by the enemy. I've got a week to perfect my excuse before I have to confront the Olds. I can stall them till Friday but then I really will have to produce the goods or face the firing squad.

Luckily, we get no results on Monday so Pete and I live to survive another day. In the meantime, we try to compare notes on realistic excuses. Unfortunately, the teachers are not being too cooperative by insisting that we turn up for class. They have to realise that this is a matter of life or death.

'Do you want to come over later?' I manage to catch Pete with his phone switched on.

'No can do, I've got to take my sister for her swimming lesson and then give her some supper,' Pete explains, 'but I'll see you tomorrow after we get some results, shall I?'

'Yep, tell your folks you're coming straight over to my place after school. Then we can sneak out into the garden without being observed,' I suggest.

Tuesday after school, we try creeping outside unobserved but Hitler's beady eyes are everywhere, 'how have you done in your exams, Peter?' she enquires.

'We haven't had any results yet, Mrs Martin,' Pete is quite relieved to reply.

'Would you two like anything to eat before I pop down to the Dry Cleaners?' She asks as she hovers.

Don't you just hate it when they hover?

'Not just now thanks, we can help ourselves if we get hungry. Come on *peter*,' by mimicking Hitler I can be sure of getting Pete's attention.

With a face as black as thunder, Pete quietly follows me out into the garden.

'You do that once more and I'll rearrange your teeth for you,' warns Pete.

'Look I want us to get away before the questions become too difficult to answer,' excusing myself at the same time as I remove my person out of Pete's sizeable reach.

'I forgive you on this occasion but make sure it does not happen again,' stresses Pete, 'shall we see if anybody is around?'

We casually saunter over to the bush in case Hitler has not succumbed to the lure of the Dry Cleaners yet. Pete has a quick recce while I keep look out. Disappointingly, nobody makes an appearance today. Tuesday and Wednesday are much the same but without the convenient visit to the Dry Cleaners.

For some unknown reason, the exam results are very delayed this year. Pete and I are naturally delighted as this gives us more breathing space but at the same time causes more anxiety with the Olds who are fast becoming extremely suspicious. This situation is testing our evasive tactics to the limit.

By Thursday we have become highly twitchy; so much so that Bud notices the moment he sets his green eyes on us.

'What on earth is the matter with you two?' he questions in amazement. Before we have the chance to reply, he gestures us to sit down and relax. As we are busy negotiating the task of attempting to squeeze us two big individuals into the confines of the bush, we are stopped dead in our tracks. Bud's companion defies belief. It really looks as if it has outgrown its bumblebee suit. Six vaguely hairy limbs and a furry head supporting two short antennae have to all intents and purposes forced their way outwards through its suit. Two huge eyes, which appear to be looking in every direction at once, dominate its head. Only when the companion rises to be formally introduced to us by Bud, do two pairs of gossamer wings unfold out from behind its back.

'You do remember Buzz?' asks Bud in a down-to-earth manner, 'he is the one responsible for the insect world.'

As if we could forget.

'So pleazzzzed to make your acquaintance,' buzzes Buzz.

We cannot tell whether Buzz is smiling or not under all that fluff. Just as we were beginning to get over the initial shock of Bud and Rep, Buzz now appears on the scene close up. Pete and I stare for the moment before we get a glimpse of each other. Boy if we thought the first two were weird, we should get an eyeful of this one. Once the second shock wave has worn off, we will be able to join in the formalities.

In the meantime, Bud takes the initiative, 'Buzz, you will recall Sam and Pete?'

Buzz buzzes his contentment at making our acquaintance again.

'Um...um.... er...' I'm struggling to find the right words here, 'are you in any way ..er..connected with bees?' I feel quite exhausted at the mental strain I put myself under to utter this question.

'Yezzzzz,' Buzz agrees, 'I am responsible for all flying insectzzzzz, to be exact. However, because of what we call the *winter squeezzzzzze* with winter starting later and finishing earlier, my work is becoming increasingly difficult. Regions such as Scotland are reporting that climate change is having an adverse effect on the seasons. Concerns are growing that many native species that are unable to adapt quickly enough will lose out to non-native species.'

'Such as?' I question.

'Butterfliezzzzz are already on the decline due to the loss of habitat and changing weather patterns but now rising temperatures cause the surviving butterfliezzzz to fly north in search of cooler weather that they are more used to. By day, we need the butterflies to pollinate the flowers; the moths take over the night shift. Unlike butterfliezzzzz, moths have ears; they can produce sound and have the ability to detect noise which enables them to fly in the dark. I notice you have nettles in your garden which make ideal food plants for the larvae. Might I suggest that you plant more flowers in your garden to help preserve the butterfliezzzz? Buddleia is a good source of nectar for the adults.'

'You might say that these are the *buzz words*, 'offers Bud with a smug look on his face. Pete and I voice our objections by groaning in perfect harmony.

'I'll mention it to my dad,' I say as if I had a clue what badlyer or whatever actually is.

'That would be thoughtful of you,' responds Buzz, 'but at this point in time, I am particularly concerned with the plight of the bee. Beezzzz, which are closely related to wasps and ants, have declined more during the twentieth century than any other insect group. The honeybee population is plummeting in the face of the ghastly parasitic varroa mite which sucks the blood from both adult and young, killing millions of them around the world. Whilst the bumblebee is also disappearing fast because of habitat loss. Beezzzz are vital pollinators of flowers, soft fruit and vegetables and are able to pollinate at lower temperatures than most insects. As the winters become milder, I have been frantically buzzing around trying to stop the beezzz from appearing too early. If they arrive before the flowers are in bloom, they will have nothing to pollinate and many plants will just die out. If the beezzz are not around, we would be unable to enjoy traditional crops such as apples, pears, plums, raspberries and strawberries.'

'I had no idea how much we depend on bees,' interrupts Pete.

'Yezzz but most alarming would be the disappearance of honey,' continues Buzz, 'I love honey; oooodlezzz of honey and it's so good for you. Did you know that you lot have used honey for over 2,000 years as an ancient remedy for infected woundzzz? Hydrogen peroxide in honey killzzz germs in the wound while amino acids and vitamin C speed the growth of healthy tissue. Honey helps woundzzz smell better too because when bacteria eat the honey they give off sweeter smelling gasezzz.'

'Yuk!' I exclaim as the very thought makes me feel sick.

'You stopped using honey with the arrival of antibioticzzz and only 30 years ago a team of your leading doctors described honey as worthlezzz and harmlezzz. Ah, but you see Big M introduces superbugzzz like MRSA resistant to antibiotics whereas honey treatment kills infections, speedzzz up healing and works against bugzzz.'

'Why do they go around stinging people?' I change the subject as I feel slightly queasy.

While he is talking, Buzz tends to move about rather a great deal. As he does so, his wings emit a continuous, monotonous, low drone. It occurs to me that if he suddenly takes off, I'm running for cover. I bet he can deliver one mighty painful sting!

'They don't only sting people; they kill other insects as well,' he continues as he meanders around, 'male beezzzz are very territorial particularly around a suitable flowering plant. If the other insectzzz refuse to be driven off, the male bee crushes the offending insect between the second and last segments of its body – rather like an insect iron maiden. Male honey beezzzz, in fact, have no sting.'

'I read somewhere that bees are lazy,' interrupts Pete.

'On the contrary,' Buzz comes right back, 'they are not like you running around like headlezzz chickenzzz. At any particular stage in a beezzzz life, it has a job to do. If it is unable to do that job it conserves its energy by doing nothing. Each bee has a unit of life energy and the faster it works, the faster it diezzz. Your very own Shakespeare in Henry V compares bee coloniezzz, in which everything works towardzzz a common aim, with a well-ordered human society.'

'Yes, Shakespeare is very observant like that,' I acknowledge in the hope that my face will not betray the fact that I haven't got a clue what Buzz is talking about and continue, ' bees aren't so bad I suppose unless they are a bit sleepy but wasps are positively aggressive.'

'Yes, I do have to keep an eye on the waspzzz otherwise you lot end up squashing them. You imagine that just because they are small and insignificant, you can kill them when you feel like it? You think you are too big to be bothered by a load of bugzzz, don't you?' Buzz adopts a more serious tone in his voice, ' well, just to prove your frailty against insectzzz, every so often Big M sends a plague of pests upon you; could be waspzzz, beezzzz, hover fliezzz, locutzzz, mosquitoezzz, the list is endlezzz. You name it; we've got it.'

'Those mossies transmit malaria;' adds doctor Pete, 'every time we go abroad my mother shovels hundreds of those anti-malaria tablets into us. Don't they also carry Vile disease?'

'It's Nile disease, to be more accurate. It's a deadly virus which can lead to severe brain complicationzzz,' Buzz wisely informs us.

'Sam won't have to worry then,' jokes Pete, 'seeing that he doesn't have much of a brain to start with.'

'Very funny, 'I sneer back at Pete. I use the welcome opportunity to shift position as it is so easy to forget just how uncomfortable and unlikely our situation is squatting under this bush since we are spellbound by what we are seeing and hearing.

'In Washington, the capital of America, for example, every 17 yearzzz the cicadas descend upon the population,' Buzz carries on regardless of the fact that another clueless expression descends upon us, 'In May of the particular year, the residentzzz of Washington DC know the invasion is coming but are powerlezzz to stop it. More than a trillion strong, with a deafening drone, which strikezzz fear into man and beast, the army of cicadas is preparing to march upwardzzz. Like an alien invasion in a 1950's low budget horror movie, this menace is known as Brood X.'

Pete and I are stumped once again. No idea what shecarders might be but instead of displaying our ignorance, we prefer to stagger on hoping Buzz will tell us sooner or later.

'You said every 17 years,' I jump in inquisitively, 'why do they wait for 17 years.'

'They are one of the world's most remarkable creaturezzz spending 17 yearzzz maturing underground before suddenly emerging as part of a vast swarm of noisy flying adultzzz. Their noise easily drownzzz out traffic, aircraft noise or the loudest music. They pozzze no threat as they do not bite, sting, or spread disease and as adult cicadazzz do not feed they do not destroy crops or plantzzz.'

'Then what's the point of sending them?' Pete asks quite reasonably.

'They make sure that their presence is felt,' Buzz clarifies the situation, ' their mindless flying meanzzz that they clumsily crash into peoples headzzz or bodiezzz; hundreds of barbecuezzz and outdoor events are ruined; against this plague insecticidezzz do work but with another billion insectzzz just around the corner to replace the ones you wipe out, the exercise is pointlezzz. By the first week of July, after each female of the brood lays her eggs maybe 500-600 in total, the adult cicadazzz will be dead and the skies silent once again. Only the lingering stench of millions of rotting insect corpsezzz will bear testament to their visit. Silently and out of sight, the whole cycle starts again until the next generation emergezzz from the ground in May 2021.'

'Creepy; can't wait,' I shiver.

'Meanwhile,' Buzz merrily hums on, 'Big M has for some time now arranged for an invasion of antzzz to menace Europe, Australia, New Zealand and more recently America. Most people think of antzzz as small and inconsequential but in Europe alone there is an army of Argentinean antzzz marching in column which stretches for 6,000 kilometrezzz. This supercolony consists of billionzzz of related ants occupying millionzzz of nests. Whereas rival ants normally fight each other to the death, these are able to recognise each other and cooperate together. To set up their nestzzz they prefer a wet environment near a food source and they eat almost anything such as meat, eggs, oils and fats. Coloniezzz are found underneath buildings, streetzzz and could even occupy your whole garden. They are now listed among the world's worst invaderzzz.'

'What's the purpose of this?' I fail to understand as I begin to itch all over.

'The purpozze?' repeats Buzz, 'whether it be tornadoezzz or termitezzz, hurricanezzz or hoverfliezzz, the purpozze is to show that however big or small, you are powerlezzzz against the force of Nature. Do you know out of interest which is the most dangerouzzz animal of all time?'

'Erm…' I am stumped temporarily by this one, 'the crocodile, I suppose?'

'Nope.'

'Man?' I blurt out feeling quite proud of myself.

'No, although I can appreciate why you would think that.'

'Erm…Oh I give up.'

'Since you are in charge of flying insects could it be one of those?' You can always rely on Pete to come up with a good suggestion.

'Well done,' Buzz congratulates Pete, 'the mosquito is responsible for the deathzzz of more human beingzz than any other creature throughout history.'

Just as we are busily trying to come to terms with this fact, Bud rises up from his seat on the rock and motions Buzz to make a move. 'At that point, we have to bid you farewell, I'm afraid,' says Bud almost with a hint of disappointment in his little voice, 'shall we have the pleasure of your company tomorrow as we could arrange to be around then?'

'We're not sure, right now,' I attempt to explain, 'only we are awaiting the results of our exams.'

'Do I detect a sense of concern?' asks Bud perceptively.

'Well, to be honest, we are not expecting good grades and our folks are going to kill us.' I reply with all the bearing of a man weighed down with the problems of life.

Bud steps forward and tells us as a gesture of comfort, 'I have told you before you must not worry. Worry is a pointless exercise. Now tell me, did you perhaps spend too much time with us and not enough on revision?'

'You did kind of take our mind off things,' stumbles Pete, 'but it's our fault we should have concentrated more on our work.'

'Trust me. You have no cause for concern,' Bud insists but before we have time to question his remark, they have both buzzed off, if you'll forgive the pun.

My mind is still churning over his words as we do our best to manoeuvre our way out from under the bush. We have done this several times now but it does not get any easier.

'What do you think he meant by that?' I quiz Pete as this continues to puzzle me.

'By what?' Pete questions.

'About us having *no cause for concern*,' I remind him in the hope that he might offer some sort of explanation.

'Oh! I think he was just being polite,' Pete seems satisfied, 'look if I don't get back soon, they'll send out a search party.'

'Incidentally, do you know why bees hum? I ask.

'No, but I expect you're going to tell me,' grumbles Pete.

'It's because they don't know the words,' I assure him.

'Before the conversation deteriorates any further, I'm off.'

'OK see you tomorrow,' I call after him.

'See you tomorrow,' Pete affirms as he cycles off into the distance in the direction of his home.

All through supper, I am unable to put Bud's words out of my mind. He is not the type to offer a clichéd remark. What am I thinking? *He is not the type*! How do I know what *type* he is? How can you categorise a moving, speaking, miniature plant that lives under a bush in my garden?

'What's up with you?' Hitler interrogates me, 'you've barely touched your food. You're not worried about your results are you?'

'No, I'm not in the least bit worried,' I lie through my teeth, 'I ate too many crisps out in the garden.'

'How many times have I told you about eating snacks before your supper?' Hitler smugly reminds me.

'Yeah! You're right. In fact, I'm feeling a bit sick, I think I'll hit the sack,' I suggest; anything to avoid the Inquisition.

Perhaps Pete is right. Bud could just have been polite but somehow I am not convinced. I am till mulling over the dilemma and as I drift off to sleep.........zzzzzzzzzz.

CHAPTER 8
A Favour Earned

Today, I am numb. I do not remember cycling to or from school. I have no recollection of actually being at school all day. It is now 4.30 on a sunny Wednesday afternoon in summer. My uniform is crumpled up with me inside it on the bed. From this I can deduce that I **must** have gone to school today. Or did I dream the whole episode?

Let me give you the facts and I'll leave you to decide. I dreamt I went to school to receive three exam results. I got straight A's for history, maths, and English. Must have been a dream. I have **never** got an A for anything; not even for turning up on time. Pete has different teachers from me for most of our subjects so I haven't seen him all day to ask what he got, otherwise I could ask him outright. I'll call him anyway; he will be able to explain my confusion.

'Hiya, what are you up to?' is all can think of to utter as I hear his voice on my mobile.

'Not much. I was thinking of coming over to your place,' Pete waits for the invite.

'How long will you be?' my mouth is way ahead of my brain.

I'll ask him face to face. Pete will know; he always has the answers to everything. I'll head him off before he encounters the Inquisitor – General. I can see him coming from my bedroom window. He is cycling so slowly down the road; he almost appears to be in slow motion. Something is definitely not right; Pete always hurtles along on his bike with his backside balanced above his saddle as if competing in the Tour de France. I wish he would give it some wellie; I am busting to find out his results. I swiftly throw on some long shorts and tee shirt to replace my dishevelled uniform. I charge down the stairs, out the front door just in time to greet Pete ambling up the garden path.

'Hiya, you took a long time to get over here,' I suggest, 'is everything OK?'

'I'm not rightly sure. How about you?' He queries but before I have chance to answer promptly, he proceeds to ask, 'did you get any results today by any chance?'

'Funny you should say that; I was just about to ask you the same question,' I am relieved to respond.

'Well?' demands Pete shrugging his shoulders while holding out his hands palms stretched upwards.

'What do you mean *well*?' I shrug back in the realisation that we **must** have gone to school today after all.

'So **did** you get any results today?' Pete impatiently raises his voice.

'Yes I did but keep your voice down or we will have company,' I urge.

'I got maths, history, and English,' Pete admits excitedly.

'So did I,' I blurt out just as enthusiastically.

'So what grades did you get?' By now there is frustration in Pete's voice.

'I…got…. straight…A's,' I empathise more to convince myself of the fact than to inform Pete.

'So did I,' confirms Pete.

'Yes but you've always had good grades. I've never got above a B before,' I attempt to impose my disbelief on Pete by asking, 'do you suppose they have made a mistake?'

'How could they have got both our grades all wrong?'

'I wasn't implying that yours were wrong; just mine,' the euphoria in my voice has dwindled somewhat.

'I haven't told my folks yet. Have you?' asks Pete.

'No, I've been avoiding them like the plague,' I assure him.

'Why? I thought you'd be pleased to give them the good news?' Pete is surprised.

'Well, no, because if there's been some sort of a mix up and I've been given somebody else's results, I'd rather wait and give them the bad news and not build their hopes up. Why on earth haven't you told yours yet?' I long to know.

'Same reason as you really. I thought I had done so badly in the exams; I can hardly believe these results. I thought I would wait until tomorrow and see what happens in the other subjects,' rationalises Pete.

'This calls for more avoidance tactics. Why don't we get some supplies from the fridge and see if anything is happening at the bush?'

'Sounds good to me,' Pete approves of my idea.

We nearly get caught rifling the fridge as I hear Hitler's car pulling into the garage but not before we mange to lay our hands on a few slices of cold roast beef, some cheese, a couple of cold baked jacket potatoes and a packet of chocolate digestive biscuits. That should keep our little friends munching for a while. Before we quickly abandon the kitchen, I have the masterstroke to leave a note advising the Olds that I have gone over to Pete's for supper. That will give us some breathing space until bedtime and with any luck we can avoid them all together this evening.

We ideally should have put this food into a bags or containers but due to lack of available scrounging time, we now have armfuls of mushy food to contend with. Not easy as we are trying to get up speed down the garden. We make a dash for the bush almost colliding in our hurry to dart underneath the spreading foliage. We narrowly avoid impact with the added risk of creating a food trifle all over the place but somehow we manage to deliver our food offerings just about in one piece. Sadly all our effort appears to have been in vain as Bud and the others fail to show.

After about two hours of hungry anticipation, we reluctantly but necessarily demolish the grub. Fed but not watered as we have not remembered to bring anything to drink plus the fact that we are beginning to feel the cold night air, we decide to abort our mission for today. We now have the tricky problem of trying to sneak back through the house without being seen or cross-examined. Pete is fortunate as he can make a quick getaway on his bike which he has cleverly secreted at the side of the house but I have to be more cunning in my efforts to escape detection. All goes according to plan; Pete heads off at a much quicker pace than his arrival with the agreement that we will meet up after school tomorrow to compare notes. I jump into bed still bewildered by today's events.

Thursday offers no relief from my state of bafflement. I have now received all my results with the exception of geography. This is nothing unusual as old *coffin dodger Brookes*, the geography master, is *always* last to mark the exam papers. He is so short sighted and decrepit that we reckon it takes him twice as long as anybody else to read anything. I digress; the point of the story is that I got A for **all** these other subjects. This just does not make sense. I did less revision this time than I have ever done, not that I have ever done much I must confess. The staff look as puzzled as I feel. I just hope that they do not think that I could have cheated. I was totally distracted throughout the exams. I could not concentrate for longer than five minutes without my thoughts wandering back to the garden.

I am beginning to smell a rat; a very kind and clever rat but an oversized rat that just happens to hang about in the bush in my garden. There I go being rude about animals; Bud is right. What have rats ever done to me? How do I know what a rat smells like? I've never smelt a rat! I've never even met one! What am I saying? *I've never met a rat.* Mind you, if I stick around long enough with the gang; I just might!

Stop thinking about rodents and focus my concentration on Bud. Exactly how he could interfere with our exam results, I cannot quite work out but I do have a sneaking suspicion that he is involved somehow. I start to gather up my things and head off home when I catch sight of Pete in the corridor.

'Pete,' I yell, 'hang on a minute.'

Pete looks round and waits for me to catch him up. I am trying a half walk, half run combination to hasten my pursuit. When you are in a hurry, your legs seem to work slower as if running in deep water; the harder you try, the target seems to get further and further into the distance. At last, I am neck and neck with Pete.

With what little breath I have left, I ask, 'how did you get on today?'

'I take it you mean my results?'

'Yeah, of course, your results. Did you think I was interested in what you had for lunch?' don't you just love sarcasm?

'I got A's for all the other subjects except geography. Old Brooksey hasn't marked it yet, not that I really care at this juncture,' Pete stares as if in a daze.

'I don't believe it! So did I. Don't you think it's suspicious?' I query.

'What do you mean suspicious?' Pete questions, 'Who or what do you suspect.'

'I can't forget Bud's words as he left us,' I state.

'What words,' asks Pete trying to remember.

'When he said that we would have nothing to worry about,' I remind him.

'How on earth could Bud have any affect on our exam results?' Pete doubts.

'I've absolutely no idea but it seemed very strange at the time.'

'Do you know what I think,' Pete gives his words of wisdom, 'I reckon you are letting your imagination run away with you.'

'Why don't we ask him, then?' I suggest

'If he turns up,' comments Pete, 'see you at your place in about half an hour.'

Simultaneously we both start to walk towards our bikes which are padlocked under the bike shed in the playground. Left foot on one pedal as we push off, closely followed by the right foot elevated over the saddle onto the opposite pedal. As I am freewheeling down our road, I am mulling over the best time and place to break the news to the Olds. It's at times like this that I really miss having grandparents around. My mum's parents passed away before I appeared on the scene; my dad's dad died when I was really small. He was married to an Italian lady, my gran, who still lives in Italy. So I have nobody to talk this over with. I am actually nervous about imparting the information to my folks. I would find it easier to tell them I'd failed the lot. I don't know how they will cope with the fact that they have a genius on their hands. Perhaps they knew all along but wanted to avoid my becoming bigheaded. I dismount; I am approaching the front door, key poised; deep breath; courage! I enter.

'Anyone home?' I call in a barely audible voice. Silence is the stern reply. Just time to change and grab some supplies for the gang and us. Great! I can hear Pete thumping on the back gate.

'Have you got everything?' he asks.

'Yes,' I confirm, 'did you get the chance to tell your folks?'

'No, I didn't stick around,' Pete is pleased to say.

'Help carry the drinks will you or I'm going to drop everything,' I dish out the orders as well as the cans of drink.

'Hand them over,' Pete's turn to do the ordering about, 'get a move on or your mum will be here before we have time to suss out the bush.'

Before we even reach the bush, we hear a familiar sound, 'I wondered how long it would take you two to arrive,' Bud's words drift our way.

'Am I glad to see you,' I let out as I attempt by ducking under the branches to see the little face that belongs to the voice.

'Sounds serious,' a frown appears on Bud's dewy countenance, 'when you are pleased to see someone, it usually implies that you want something from them.'

'That's a very cynical comment,' I suggest.

'Well, cynics never get disappointments or surprises,' Bud offers his words of reason, 'how did you fare with your exams?'

'That's the very thing we wanted to have words about,' I am busting to have the chance to speak, 'before we left you last time you said that we would have nothing to worry about. What did you mean by that?'

'Exactly what I said,' Bud states in his straightforward tone.

'We both passed every exam at A grade except geography which we are still waiting for,' I exclaim

'And you're complaining?' queries Bud, somewhat amazed.

'Not complaining, just surprised,' I tell him, 'I've never had an A grade before for any subject. Pete has but I never have.'

'I still do not understand your problem,' Bud now seems quite bemused.

'Did you have anything to do with this?' I stammer out swiftly.

'A favour earned, is a favour returned,' Bud quotes at us.

'I've not heard that quote before?' Pete questions.

'No, I do believe that I am the author,' admits Bud as a hint of a feint smile adorns his budlike face which is slightly dipped in a display of embarrassed pride. I try to work out whether he is blushing but it is very difficult bearing in mind his peculiar colouring.

'What does it mean? Who did the favour?' I am dying of curiosity.

'Firstly, we want to thank you for keeping our little secret to yourselves,' Bud's shrill voice expresses their gratitude.

'How do you know we haven't told anybody?' I challenge him.

'Otherwise there would be hordes of sticky beaks here by now all peering under the bush trying to catch a fleeting glimpse of us,' Bud asserts confidently, 'that aside, you are both very kind in bringing us food, particularly as it must be difficult for you to sneak out of the house bearing armfuls of tasty morsels,' Bud explains, 'so we and by that I include all the others, especially Big M are truly grateful for your consideration. Big M is not called **Mother** Nature for nothing, you know.'

'Could Big M come one day by any chance?'

'You mean here?'

'Yeah?'

'Oh no, she's far too busy. She has to be everywhere, all of the time that's why she enlists our help but I'll mention that you asked after her.'

'I nearly forgot, we brought these for you,' I hastily interrupt as we unravel from our persons our warm and squashed offerings which we proceed to hand over to them.

'That's most kind of you,' Bud thanks us sincerely and continues, 'at first we could not decide how to reward your generosity. We wanted to make a gesture which would demonstrate our appreciation. We had to select an action which would be specifically relevant to you two.'

'So what did you do?' Pete stops Bud in his tracks.

'If you will kindly allow me to finish, all will be revealed,' Bud asserts his position, 'we arranged for you to study successfully for your exams.'

'How on earth did you manage that?'

'By means of *mindvision* which I believe you call *mindsight,* Bud advises us.

'I'm still none the wiser,' I retort.

'As I said all will be revealed in due course,' states Bud, 'now I really must be gone. I have so much that needs my urgent attention. So for now, I bid you farewell.'

And he is gone.

'You can't leave us like this,' I try a little blackmail but to no effect, 'I do wish he wouldn't just up and go like that.'

'It is maddening,' agrees Pete, 'but I guess we'll just have to wait till next time; if there is a next time?'

CHAPTER 9
Tortellini Torture

My annual four-week sentence at my gran's in Italy is usually agony but this year it is sheer torture. I now find myself in the middle of nowhere without any of my life-sustaining distractions.

On the minus side:
I have no Pete
I have no iPod
I have no YouTube
I have no Facebook
I have no bush to hide under
I have no Gang
I have my Gran
I have Hitler
I have Italian television
I have the dopey dog to annoy
I have my mobile which I can use under penalty of death

On the plus side:
I have been here for two days so far and already I am losing the will to live.

I am truly alone.

I thought that this year I would have been taken somewhere special as a reward for my *once in a lifetime; never to be repeated; fantastic* exam results. At the very least, I should have been granted a reprieve. My four weeks should have been commuted to one week, maybe two for good behaviour. To add insult to injury, the Old Man arrives in a fortnight. Now why doesn't that cheer me up? That thought has now made me completely lose the will to live.

Can you believe that Hitler insists upon driving **all the way** here; except the bit across the Channel naturally? She claims that we need the car to get about as gran lives miles from anywhere. Has she not heard that they hire cars in Italy? It's revolutionary and highly unusual, I will admit. Instead we have to travel in the Nissan Cherry which has a sunroof that leaks if we turn right when it rains. So as long as we plan our journey which involves only making left turns we don't get wet. The go faster stripes, which once shone brightly along the edge of the doors, have been replaced by going even faster rust! To further increase the agony, Hitler is bad enough driving on the left hand side of the road but once we switch to the right, scary!! She drives **so** slowly. Some cars travel from nought – to – sixty in six seconds, Hitler does it in an hour and a half! She drives too slowly to have an accident but I reckon she causes hundreds! Just wait till I can drive, I'll show them how to handle a car. Throughout the lengthy ordeal, I try to keep her spirits up with encouraging remarks like *are we there yet?* Or *the dog's been sick again.* We must possess the only hound that's travelsick. It's a relief that we have already passed through immigration otherwise the officers would not have recognised our green Dalmatian from the photo in the doggy passport. I am not sure how many weeks or months the journey takes but eventually we arrive in sunny Solto Collina.

I unfold out of the back of the car which is stupidly designed with only two doors at the front. I get out gingerly just in case the prolonged concertina effect on my body has impaired my ability to walk. No, I can stand; the numbness will hopefully wear off in time. Gran greets us enthusiastically as always at the door of her casa. She always wears her long black skirt with her shawl draped loosely over her rounded shoulders. I doubt she ever removes her small rimless glasses perched on the tip of her nose. She never looks through them but always peers over the top to see anything.

The goats, Lazlo and Eric (pronounced Ereeck), I forgot to the mention the goats, shuffle out to see if anything is edible. They will even munch on the luggage given half a chance. They are solid brutes standing nearly as tall as Spot. Patches of white fur squeeze through here and there on their predominately black coats. They amble over to greet us but their interest in anything lasts only as long as their appetites will allow. Spot rumbles towards the goats to sniff out his new playmates but is very soon discouraged by their rapidly flicking tails and sharp display of horns.

'Ciao, Bella,' croaks Gran as she wraps herself around mother.
'Ciao, Bella,' muffles mother as she disappears beneath gran's shawl.

ɔy waiting for my slobbery kiss which is part
ʳelcoming ritual. It is not too long before I too
am enveloped in her vast net of goat's wool at risk
from either suffocation or slow death by itching.

'Ciao Bella.'
'Ciao Bella.'

I call my gran 'Bella' as she says *bella* to everything.
That is the extent of my Italian. I don' speaka da
lingo. My Gran don' speaka no Inglese. Hitler tries a
version of Italianised English which is really
laughable. Can't see the point of adding the pressure
of learning another language just for four weeks
each year; I struggle with English. Communication is
kept to a minimum which is probably for the best in
all honesty. Besides what do you say to a sweet little
wizened old prune that is not in touch with reality?
On the bright side, gran is a very good cook.
However, after four weeks there is just so much
penne, fussilli, spaghetti, or tortellini that a 14 year
old genius of the male variety can consume.

Gran lives some distance away from the centre of
Solto Collina in an old farm house. Attached to the
rear of the house is a garden and to the side are two
vast olive groves long since disused as gran has
lived alone for a number of years. She has been a
widow ever since I have known her and her two sons
moved abroad so she didn't have the money to hire
anybody to work for her. I don't remember my
granddad as he died way back in history long before

I was even thought of. Gran fondly describes him as tall, dark and handsome bearing a striking resemblance to dad. I think time has faded her memory and her eyesight. Questions about what to do with the land after gran bites the dust have been on my parent's lips of late.

However, they need fear no more. Even gran is in a state of excitement at recent events which could prove fatal at her grand age. Suddenly there has been an explosion of building around Solto Collina of holiday houses and apartments for rent or to buy. The glossy brochures now advertise '*luxury properties available in or near the historic centre of Solto Collina, a small medieval village with panoramic views from the hillside overlooking the placid Lake Iseo.*' Agreed if you happen to like balancing on the edge of dirty great big hills staring down at vast expanses of water without getting the urge to hurtle yourself over the edge, then this is the place for you. Obviously there are a lot of suckers around. Where gran lives is still rural and not much of a going concern but not for much longer by the look of things. Reckon I'll have to learn to like the shawl-smothering from now on.

So I while away the time in my gran's garden constantly churning over Bud's words in my mind. I am dying of curiosity wondering how he did what he did. How could he possibly affect our exam results? Perhaps he hypnotised us? I am going to go crazy in four weeks. Thank goodness, there is a lot of garden to while away the time and go crazy in. The land is vast; you can't see your neighbours. It is so vast you can't even see your neighbours with binoculars. The only problem is that if you do not have a passion for veggies, the garden will not hold much appeal. Out back of the farmhouse or should I now say the villa is one huge vegetable patch. I suppose people of my gran's generation are very thrifty having survived two world wars but she is also miles from any shops. There is a small cafe just a short distance away which is run by Luigi and his fourth wife. He apparently collects wives like other people save stamps. My gran reckons they all died of hard work. The amazing thing is if you can you imagine this, my gran has *never* been to a restaurant, café or bar in her whole 86 years on this Earth? She argues that they only serve pasta and she can cook that better at home. Makes sense if you think about it.

By the fourth day, I am toying with the idea of creating my own ancient Roman games. I can pitch Lazlo against Eric who can lock horns in glorious battle. The winner can take on Spot. As the Emperor, I can decide by the mere gesture of my thumb up or down whether the contest was fair and exciting enough for the four-legged gladiators to live or die. My Imperial plans are cut short by Hitler who announces that we are shortly going out to visit some of my gran's friends that she hasn't seen for yonks. Gran doesn't drive; never learnt to and there is no public transport in the area so she does not go out much. This is going to be fun!

We are on our way to a small village called Sotto

il Monte, a small country village in the Province of Bergamo, which is famous as the birthplace of Pope John Paul XX111. This tiny village hasn't changed much since the days when the young future Pope was brought up by his family of sharecroppers. The village, still inhabited mainly by frugal peasant farmers, has all the tourist attractions of Solto Collina plus a shop which sells absolutely everything you could possibly think of. The local hot spot is Paulo's Taverna which boasts a bar with a television that regularly shows the UEFA cup football matches!! Sadly, we drive straight past the Taverna as Hitler begins to negotiate a non-existent dirt track off to the left immediately after the shop. She likes to pretend she's driving her *Chelsea Tractor,* one of those giant four-wheel drive, off-the-road vehicles, instead of clapped out old Japanese junk. This is worse than turbulence on a plane. I am being buffeted from one side of the back seat to the other. How gran manages to sleep through this ordeal is beyond me. She is slumped in the passenger seat with her head bobbing up and down like one of those *nodding dogs* that people use to decorate the rear window of their car. Yet as if by radar, she wakes up the minute we arrive at the Antonellis.

I then have to endure two whole hours in Mario and Maria's kitchen pretending to enjoy myself. I have only a glass of weak orange juice and a miserable biscuit to see me through constant verbal attacks in croaky Italian. They rabbit so quickly and forcefully that if they weren't smiling I could swear they were being rude. At one point, Hitler gets up and my heart

121

leaps anticipating our imminent departure but my joy is short-lived as she is only going to the toilet. Two hours, twenty minutes and hundreds of arrivedercis later, we finally make a move. Gran is so elated by the whole experience that on the journey home she succeeds in staying awake for a full ten minutes before she nods off again.

The next day, the excitement has obviously taken its toll on gran as she does not surface till after 6 a.m.!! As a rule, if you are not down by 7, you've missed breakfast. This is the only meal that does not consist of pasta and tomato sauce. Cornflakes are alright but not soaked in goat's milk. According to gran, it's supposed to be healthier for you than cow's milk. The problem is that it smells of goats and I have no desire to end up reeking of goat's cheese together with risking sprouting horns and a beard. Breakfast over, now comes the task of busying myself until lunch.

I spend today and the next few days happily drifting in and out of boredom. I wish to savour these moments for as long as humanly possible as the Old Man arrives tomorrow to begin his annual two-week sabbatical. For these forgettable fourteen days, Slowpoke Pecos emerges from his chrysalis and transforms himself into Action Man. Ground Force comes to Solto Collina. He spends hours messing about with the vegetables though gran wishes he wouldn't. He thinks his fingers are greener than the Jolly Green Giant's. In point of fact, he hasn't got a clue so between them the two women figure out ruses to keep him otherwise occupied. Long, healthy walks are one way of preserving the veggies from his manic digging. He enjoys trips to this Sotto place as he can pop into the bar while he is there. So Hitler and gran contrive endless lists of supplies that have mysteriously run out all of a sudden. Nobody is quite sure whether he is aware of their cunning plan since he never complains about the number of visits he has to make to Sotto. It's strange that back home he hates going to the shops but here he positively seems to relish his shopping sprees. I somehow get route marched into the long, healthy walks but am oddly overlooked for the Sotto bashes.

Monday is all thrills here as the vet is coming to check out the goats as they have lost their appetites. I realise something is up when I can't even tempt them with my school bag. Normally, this would make a tasty morsel for a hungry goat. I am even prepared to dowse it with pasta sauce but they turn up their beards at this generous offer. If they get so much as an inkling of their impending doom, they will scarper. So we will have to persuade, cajole, entice or if all else fails, force them into their pen before the vet arrives.

For a little guy in a smart suit, the vet displays a lot of pluck. It takes courage to face two angry and hungry goats that are confined unwillingly inside a small pen. Signor Capelli strolls into the pen as large as life clutching his battered black bag close to his side. He starts rambling off in coochy coochy Italian in an attempt to calm the savage beasts. As soon as he stretches out his hand to stroke Laslo the whiff of hypodermic reaches their nostrils and they go berserk. Amid a barrage of kicking, butting and bleating, Signor Vet makes a quick exit out of the pen. He issues some instructions to my gran while his hands make gestures in my direction. I rapidly begin to lose interest in the situation as I know what's coming!

'He wants you to hold on the goats so that he can give them a flu jab,' Hitler informs me.

'In your dreams,' I mutter under my breath. 'I don't know how to hold a goat,' I protest out loud.

'Now's your chance to learn. In you go with the vet,' Hitler is not standing for any nonsense.

They want me, a confirmed coward, to enter an enclosed space to face two crazed goats. Do I look insane or something?

I find myself being ushered forward by my father's fist in the small of my back. Why doesn't he boldly go where only the vet has boldly gone before? What do you say to two barmy Italian goats? Even if I could communicate with them, I doubt somehow at this precise moment that they would be interested in the fact that I hate injections as well. Don't The Olds care that I might be facing possible injury for life? The light of their only son and heir might be extinguished forever? As the gate is shut behind me I realise that they couldn't care less.

'Here Lazlo. Here Eric,' I extend my hand towards the manic brutes wishing I knew which goat was which. The vet indicates that he wants me to grab one of them by the horns, as you do! I decide my only hope is to imagine myself taking part in a Wild West Rodeo. So here I go, the Italian version of John Wayne indulging in not steer but goat wrestling. This cannot be right; I am spending more time on the ground than the goats. There is as much commotion going on outside the pen as there is inside. I'm shouting and screaming as I am persistently being dumped in the dirt. Meanwhile, the ringside spectators are all yelling their various instructions with the exception of gran who is croaking in Italian. They are making such a din that it's hard to tell whether they are offering advice or placing bets on the outcome. What would Pete do in a situation like this I begin to wonder? Knowing Pete, he would never have allowed himself to get into a mess like this in the first place. Pete would probably dive into a rugby tackle but then I played football. I swiftly swap from cowboy to gladiator and remove my top. I, Samus Gladiatorus, bare-chested in true gladiatorial style wrap my tee shirt around my forearm. I face the goats square on. Like a matador now, I unravel the tee shirt and tease the goats with it. While they are in a state of confusion, I manage to throw my top over the head of one of the goats so I am able to pull the beast onto the ground. Just when I think I have successfully secured the ungrateful animal in a hammerlock grip, it bites my arm.

'Ow,' I scream out in pain.

'What's the matter?' Hitler calls.

'That rotten beast has made a meal of my arm,' I yell back at her as I witness the blood oozing down my forearm.

'Well, never mind, the vet has managed to inoculate them both,' she says to cheer me up. What does she mean *never mind?* Here am I with a hole in my arm which was not there but five minutes ago and my life's blood is dripping away. Now to add insult to injury she suggests, 'perhaps we can get the vet to have a look at your arm?'

That's all I need, to be examined by a goat doctor. Still it's better than bleeding to death. Signor Capelli puts a tourniquet around the top of my arm as he covers the bite with an adhesive strip. I could wittily joke that *one good tourniquet deserves another* but nobody appears to be in the mood for merriment especially me when the vet decides I need a tetanus jab. Blood loss I can handle but a tetanus needle that's a different kettle of pesce. The very thought fills me with dread. If he reckons he has had problems darting the goats, he ain't seen nothing yet!

'I had one last year when I fell off my bike on the way to school. The school nurse gave it to me,' I promise. 'I don't remember that,' doubts Hitler.

'Well, it's true and you're not supposed to have them too often,' I'll blind them with science. They seem to swallow it and the vet removes the tourniquet so that my circulatory system can return to normal before my arm drops off.

'Grazie! Grazie,' warbles gran as she grabs me in a bear hug.

'It was nothing,' I fearlessly smirk. All in a day's work for us heroes. Is there no end to my talents? Exam Whiz Kid at school; Now Italian Goat Champion. Wait till I tell Pete that I am the local hero in these parts. I bet he won't believe me.

After all this excitement, we are tired and hungry so gran invites the vet to stay for supper. I toy with the idea of telling him that goat is on the menu but decide against it just in case he reaches for the tetanus vaccine. Although I could have done without my arm being half chewed off, this interlude has livened the old place up.

The remainder of the holiday seems quite dull after the goat episode. My thoughts rapidly return to Pete, Bud and the bush. Going home can't come soon enough.

After a few more sorties to Sotto and several more pasta meals later, we are finally loading up the Batmobile for the long journey home. We call the car by the same name as Batman's super vehicle simply because it is black and has four wheels, apart from that the resemblance is strikingly different. On the way back, I have to contend with having the Old Man in the car. By this I mean that any junk that travelled out on the front passenger seat will now have to be accommodated in the rear beside me. To further add to my misery, gran thoughtfully loads us up with fresh veggies straight from her garden. The car looks like a mobile greenhouse. The boot is full; the front seats are occupied; we do not have a roof rack which is probably a blessing in disguise as the rust might collapse under the weight; there is but one place for all the ballast that's on the back seat with the luggage, the dog and me. With half a botanical garden next to me I could start my own Eden Project. Coming out it was cramped, going back it is agony.

By the time we arrive back hundreds of light years later, I am not too sure that I will reach my full height ever again. I hobble inside the house and immediately call Pete.

'See you tomorrow,' he thankfully agrees. I imagine Pete and his family have been somewhere exotic for their holiday. They usually do. This time I'll have some fascinating tales of my own to tell. I can't wait for the morning.

CHAPTER 10
Mindvision

Pete comes rolling over about 8.30 in the morning. Normally I would moan that it is far too early in the holidays but oddly today, I am wide-awake. I thought the journey would have shattered me but I am up and raring to go. I want to slip outside unnoticed but Hitler has to start rabbiting to Pete as soon as she lays eyes on him.

'Have you been away, Peter?' she annoyingly asks.

'Yes, Mrs Martin, we went to Disney World in Florida,' cheerfully replies Pete. She would have to ask wouldn't she although this year I am not as green with envy as usual. Wait till Pete hears my heroic stories.

'How are your parents? Did they enjoy their holiday,' Hitler persists with stupid questions. What does she expect Pete to answer? *No, they had a rotten time?*

'Yes,' confirms Pete, 'in fact, they want to go again next year.' Perhaps if I ask often enough they might consider taking me along? Well, I can dream, can't I?

'Why don't we go outside and you can tell me all about it?' I prompt. After the stories of the themed hotel, the new rides, and the food, at long last, Pete takes the hint and we wander out into the jungle.

'What's all this you mentioned yesterday when you called about you wrestling with goats? It's not like your one about Micro Beings under a bush is it?' there is a touch of sarcasm in Pete's voice which I can't say that I enjoy.

'Ha! Ha! Very funny,' I sneer, 'no my gran's two goats had to be inoculated against goat flu and I was the only one brave enough to assist the vet. I even got I injured in the process.' Whereupon, I roll up my sleeve to reveal the imprints that either Eric or Lazlo's teeth left in my arm.

'Wow! That looks painful,' Pete seems impressed.

'Hardly noticed a thing,' I proudly boast

Whilst we are strolling and engrossed in conversation, we reach the bush before we realise it. Despite the fact that it is a bit overcast today, we can still get a clear view under the bush. We cautiously peer underneath to reveal Bud as usual perched upon something and today it is a small log. What we are not prepared for is his companion. It is the stony looking one with the permanently furrowed brow.

'Welcome. Welcome,' invites Bud, 'I am so pleased you have come today as I want you to get to know Rodie.'

Pete and I struggle to meander under the foliage in an attempt to make ourselves comfortable for today's episode in the saga whilst at the same time our eyes

remain transfixed upon this member of the group.
Rodie's marblesque tone gives a touch of unreality to
his appearance. As if this whole situation is in any
way, shape or form linked to the real world but Rodie
is like a statue newly dislodged from its plinth.

'How do you do?' the statue speaks. The deep
sound of his voice together with the worried look on
his face combine to add a note of genuine concern
about the question.   A reply of *fine thanks* might
indicate an air of flippancy.

So as not to appear rude, I hastily scramble my
thoughts together and utter, 'we are both well, thank
you for asking.' What a lame response!

'Allow me to tell you a little more about Rodie's role
in the organisation,' Bud senses our unease and
quickly takes the matter in hand, 'he does all the
thinking around here. He assesses matters in order
of priority and it is up to me to delegate them as soon
as possible.'

'I hate to be difficult but we were rather hoping that
you could shed some light on the little matter of you
helping us with our exams,' I have to get this off my
chest as this has been on my mind ever since we got
our brilliant grades.

'Oh, the impatience of Youth. What is the rush?'
contemplates Bud as he emits a deep sigh, 'very
well, I will try to explain. Have you ever been thinking
about somebody that you haven't seen for ages and

out of the blue they call you? Have you ever heard of incidences of animals knowing in advance just when their owners are about to arrive?'

'Yes,' answers Pete, 'it's called coincidence.'

'Well, over the years these coincidences have been justified by a number of different explanations,' responds Bud, 'at varying times, these have been called telepathy, intuition, extra sensory perception or simply good luck. Call it what you will but we are all anxious to believe in supernatural powers, in fate or in destiny as this saves us from having to take responsibility for ourselves. That's why horoscopes are so popular. As I told you previously, you have chosen to christen this phenomenon mindsight but we prefer mindvision. Sight is defined as the power of seeing whereas vision is the manner of perceiving but in this case not with the eyes but with the mind.'

'What exactly is it?' I question as I fear I am losing the plot.

'We have learned to enhance and use our seventh sense,' states Bud in quite a matter-of-fact way.

'Hold it just one cotton-picking moment. I thought we had **five** senses,' I dare to suggest.

'No we actually possess more, we just haven't yet learned how to use them,' insists Bud.

'Well, if we accept that, what happened to the sixth sense?'

'Here, I will hand you over to Rodie,' Bud smiles and turns towards his companion who does not appear to have the inclination to get restless.

The statue rises up to his full height of about 46cm give or take a few bits of plaster, adjusts his toga to accommodate respectability and bursts forth with surprising animation. I grant you it's very difficult to imagine an animated lump of concrete but it's no easier when you're staring at it.

'Before I go onto the sixth and seventh senses can you tell me what your five senses are?' Rodie enquires.

'Easy,' we reply in unison, 'Seeing, hearing, smelling,' we rattle off and then the pace slows down, 'um...now don't tell us it's on the tip of our tongues...um...feeling, that's it, and......'

Bud moves forward as if to put us out of our misery.

'No, it's just coming,' Pete becomes our spokesperson when he suddenly has a flash of inspiration, 'tasting,' he lets out with a sigh of relief.

'Well done,' Rodie praises our efforts before adding, 'to be more exact they are sight, taste, touch, smell and hearing but you basically named them correctly.'

We are feeling quite proud of ourselves which probably shows all over our faces.

'As a matter of fact, all your senses work together by sending messages to your brain, 'proclaims Rodie enthusiastically, 'so if you lose one of your senses the others often compensate for the loss; sometimes these other senses even develop to the point that they become far more efficient.'

'Is that the same with the sixth and seventh senses?' I chip in.

'Not quite,' says Rodie, 'our sixth sense is how we communicate with feelings which is what some people call intuition. Do you know what this means?'

'Is that when you think something is going to happen but you can't explain why?' Pete offers.

'In a way, yes,' Rodie confirms, 'our sixth sense is our feelings and how we communicate with them. It allows us to get information through our feelings. You know how you sometimes sense something is going to happen or you understand how somebody is feeling without even speaking to them?'

'Is that what you call empathy?' asks Pete.

'I am impressed,' admits Rodie.

That makes three of us!

'So what's the seventh then?' I step in.

'Our seventh sense is the way in which we use our intelligence through thought,' Rodie puts it into plain words.

'Not sure I'm with you there,' I hate to own up to the fact that I'm a bit lost.

'OK our seventh sense is our ability to communicate through thought; is that any clearer?' Rodie makes it easier.

'You mean like ESP?' now it's my turn to look intelligent.

'Or to give it the full title,' intercepts Rodie, 'extrasensory perception.'

You can just feel the telepathy or whatever you want to call it suddenly flitting between Pete and me.

'Well, the mind has powers that can reach out and affect other people,' admits Bud, 'in fact, when one person concentrates on another, it can actually cause a measurable rise in blood pressure. This explains the familiar belief that the sensation of burning ears means someone is talking about you.'

'Why can't we do this,' asks Pete.

'You human beings have taken thousands of years to get rid of your ability to communicate telepathically because such powers would actually lessen your chances of survival in a modern city. Telepathy operates best in a deeply relaxed state and such a state would increase your chances of having or causing an accident,' Rodie takes up the story from here.

'You mean to say that once upon a time we had these telepathic powers?' I am staggered.

'Shall I carry on?'

At this point, Rodie turns to Bud to make sure that he is not out of order.

'If you would be so kind,' Bud indicates in an authoritative and yet gracious manner.

'Yes, indeed,' Rodie burst forth once more, 'your ancient ancestors knew the importance of having a seventh sense which alerted them to the approach of enemies or wild animals. They even had someone who specialised in doing it for the benefit of the tribe. He was known as the shaman or medicine man and they relied on him to protect the others by using his powers to warn them of danger while they got on with the practical business of hunting or agriculture.'

'Does anybody still have these powers?'

'There was a remarkable Englishman in the early part of the twentieth century called Jim Corbett who spent most of his life hunting man-eating tigers in

India whereby he found himself developing an interesting faculty,' Rodei is in full flow now and thoroughly enjoying recounting his tales, 'he called it *jungle sensitiveness* which he claimed time and again saved his life when a tiger was lying in wait.'

'Yeah but we don't come across too many tigers around these parts,' you can always rely on us for the smart reply.

'Have you never heard of incidences when people, for example, miss the flight that they are scheduled to take only to discover afterwards that the plane had crashed?' Rodei illustrates, 'some of you have an enhanced seventh sense. Sometimes you just *feel* that something is wrong and often it is. Other times you just *know* that someone in your family is in trouble.'

'Ah we see what you mean,' we stand corrected and hang on to his every word.

'This sense is more developed in some than in others. Sometimes this can be hereditary due to genetic variations or it could be a gender difference. Intuition tends to be more evolved in females,' Rodie reveals.

'You can say that again. My mother can smell a rat ooops sorry, she knows instinctively if we are up to no good.'

At which point, both Bud and Rodei fix me with a scornful stare whilst contemplating whether to persevere or not. I shift about awkwardly as I can see that even Pete wishes to disown me. As the ground will not oblige by opening up to swallow me whole, I feel my face turning bright crimson in total harmony with my hair. When the pair feels that my degree of embarrassment is sufficient, a sharp nod from Bud signals the official seal of approval for Rodei to continue.

'We also possess very highly enhanced vision known as tetrachromatic through which we are able to distinguish between two variations of the same shade of colour. While many of your men are colour blind to some extent or other a few women have this enhanced vision,' Rodei confides, 'on the whole, you have no need for jungle sensitiveness or enhanced vision or telepathic powers but this knowledge has been acquired over millions of years. It is a skill that lies just below the surface and the important thing to learn is how easy it is to make use of it.'

'Is **that** how you influenced our exam results?'

'We did nothing of the kind,' insists Bud, 'we merely acted as the sender and you were the receiver. By concentrating on you we were able to send you a simple Morse Code message. We just encouraged you to be positive about your abilities; the rest was up to you.'

'So you could do it again another time?' I suggest hopefully.

'We could in theory but we won't,' declares Bud,' we have returned the favour. Besides if you have succeeded once what's to stop you repeating the process? Just remember what you did last time.'

'I don't even recall doing it; never mind doing it again!'

'You **must** remember,' insists Bud, 'we are but memory; without memory, we cease to exist. Memory reminds us how to speak, eat, walk and think; everything we have ever learned is stored in our memory; if this fails you are no longer a living being. But we don't want to leave you on that scary note; what do you think is your most valuable sense?'

'Sight,' I reckon, 'as you can see nice things as well as danger.'

'Hearing,' disagrees Pete, 'so you can hear people talking and music.'

'These are all very vital,' Bud accepts, 'but the most important is your sense of humour and you two have plenty of that. People with a negative outlook on life are more likely to be ill and unhappy. Laughter is a medicine which is free, fun and anyone can use it.'

We have been so completely captivated by the proceedings and have failed to notice that the time has flown. Before hunger or mother come looking for us, we politely make our excuses to leave. Bud and Rodie appear satisfied and pleased with their day's work. As Pete and I struggle to remove ourselves from the bush and wake up our legs from their enforced slumber, we are left with a feeling of amazement and confusion. We stroll back to the house in silence.

CHAPTER 11
Forest Pharmacy

Typical British summer! It hasn't stopped pouring down for two whole days. That's forty-eight hours of valuable garden time lost to the squelch. Pete and I have been confined to either his house or mine or, to be more precise, to his bedroom or mine. In his room he has his own telly and furthermore any empty space is not compressed by rows of rotten books. On the other hand, my place has the added advantage that we can, hopefully, escape Pete's sister Emily who has become obsessed with pestering us all the time. This brings with it an added complication in the shape of her friend, Charlie, who just happens to have taken a liking to **me**. I suppose she is not bad as girls go but I wish she would **go,** preferably as far away as possible.

To make matters worse, Pete's mum keeps **insisting** that we drag the two girls along with us everywhere. They persist in interrupting us when we are busy. Charlie goes all soppy and fiddles with her long, curly hair. She follows me around like some lost puppy. She does everything I tell her. Sit Charlie! Stand Charlie! And she obeys. I am sure that if I told her to go and lay face down in the mud, she would but I don't. For a start her mother would most likely kill me for ruining her new dress. Why can't girls amuse themselves like us? These two are old enough to be a nuisance.

There are presently four bodies plonked on my bed flattening the duvet. Outside it looks at long last as if the rain is going to stop and it might brighten up. Two of us are coyly fiddling with our curls or showing off our matching pink and white gingham outfits while the other two of us are concentrating hard on humane methods of pest control. How to rid ourselves of a pair of giggling, chattering and annoying individuals without causing life-threatening injuries? Pete and I desperately want to wander outside to see what we might discover today under the bush. There is no way we are going to have Tweedledum and Tweedledee dragging along. Can you just imagine the commotion? It's bad enough with the dog around but with these two noisy objects hanging onto us everywhere we go it doesn't bear thinking about. No, we are going to have to employ cunning avoidance tactics.

'Doesn't your mother want you back home for lunch?' I casually suggest. Now I wouldn't have thought that this is a particularly amusing question but it evokes ripples of giddy laughter from the chequered duo. I carry on regardless and decide to try a more simple approach.

'Aren't you getting hungry?' A suggestion which turns embarrassed expressions bright pink in perfect harmony with the dresses but provokes no verbal response from the couple of hyenas. Pete and I glare at each other whilst simultaneously blowing sighs of frustration. I raise my eyebrows at Pete in an appeal for help and support here. Fortunately he senses my desperation and leaps into action.

'Come on you two, it's about time I got you back. Your mothers will be wondering where you have got to,' he says as he skilfully ushers the two ankle biters out of the bedroom and down the stairs. We almost make a clean getaway when Hitler bars our escape route out the front door.

'Where do you think you are going?' she demands knowing full well that she has foiled our plan.

'We thought that that the girls would be feeling hungry and we ought to be getting them back home,' offers Pete.

'That's very considerate of you but their mothers have asked me to look after them until this evening as they are going shopping together,' she informs us in no uncertain terms and much to our dismay.

I have a sudden brainwave, 'so where are you taking them? ' I smile in cheeky anticipation.

'Nice one,' is her stern reply.

Drats, she hasn't fallen for my ploy!!

'I will make some lunch for everybody and then it will be up to you two boys to entertain Emily and her friend this afternoon,' she continues before turning to the girls, 'your dresses are very pretty. I bet they were expensive.'

'Oh no, mum didn't pay for them,' Charlie's innocent remark leaves a puzzled look on Hitler's face.

'She didn't?' quizzes Hitler.

'No,' comes Charlie's positive response spoken with all the matter-of-fact charm of one so young, 'she used a credit card.' At this comment Hitler's expression relaxes into one of relieved disbelief. She smiles quite noticeably as she opens the fridge door.

We all sit round the kitchen table munching away at our lunch. Pete and I sit in dejected silence. Even the food gives us no consolation. Chips and beans *might* have helped to lift our spirits a little but what good is cold pasta salad to the downhearted? Ever since we returned from Italy, Hitler has diligently, if not successfully, worked her way through the *100 Things to do with Pasta* recipes. I could suggest my 101st idea but I would probably be grounded for life!

If we can manage to prolong lunch for an hour at least, we can shorten the agony time this afternoon. Hitler, however, has other intentions. No sooner have the last mouthfuls left their forks than the plates are whipped away at breakneck speed to be deposited in the dishwasher. It is now very apparent that our welcome like the food in the kitchen has run out.

'You two like spending time in the garden so off you go,' commands Hitler, 'and make sure that the girls do not spoil their new dresses. Oh and by the way, don't let the dog dig up your father's nasturtiums.' Whereupon, Pete, me, nuisances one and two plus the flaming hound are railroaded outside.

'That's not fair,' I protest loudly, 'you didn't say anything about looking after the dog as well.'

'I can't take him with me to the dentist. The only dogteeth he treats are mine,' she smirks.

So we find ourselves completely at a loss. We have to restrain Spot from digging up the miserable plants and venturing near the bush just in case the walking tablecloths become inquisitive. This is going to be a real test of our ingenuity.

'How about hide and seek?' chimes up Emily.

'No!' Pete and I yell in unison, realising that if they choose to hide under *the* bush we could have a catastrophe on our hands.

'There's no need to shout,' the girls object with a hint of sulking thrown in.

'Sorry,' I hastily apologise, 'we were just a bit worried that you might spoil your nice outfits if you got tangled up in the bushes.' They appear to be satisfied with my explanation but this still does not solve our problem. Pete suggests that we go for a

145

walk to the local newsagent to get some ice creams as we really need to get the girls out of the garden. This idea is greeted with enthusiasm but before we can put the plan into action, the stupid dog goes bounding straight for the bush. He immediately starts digging to the accompaniment of a chorus of whining and barking; his weird behaviour naturally stirs up the curiosity of the gingham pair.

'What's the matter with Spot?' asks Charlie.

'Nothing, he is looking for somewhere to go to the toilet,' the words spurt out of my mouth in quick succession. I hope that this will deter the girls from following the dog to investigate.

'Yuk!' cries Emily in disgust.

'Urgh!' echoes Charlie.

It seems to have had the desired effect as the pink and white twins shuffle back towards the house. I have hidden Spot's lead in my pocket for if he even suspects that he is about to be attached to it, he will bunk. Before I can execute this delicate operation, luck turns our way. Mother unexpectedly comes out of the house to explain that her appointment has been cancelled as the dentist is off sick with the flu. Whoopee! The dentist's loss is our gain. Mother offers to take the girls to the park with the dog. We cannot believe our good fortune.

'Are you sure?' I check, 'we were looking forward to taking the girls to get an ice cream.'

'Don't push your luck,' warns Hitler, 'we'll go to the pond near the playground and feed the ducks.'

As soon as they are out of sight, Pete and I make straight for the bush.

'You took your time,' grumbles Bud, 'I thought you would never get here.'

'Sorry,' I apologise, 'we just could not get rid of Pete's sister and her friend.'

Bud sits there with a grin on his face in spite of his moans he is evidently pleased to see us. Meanwhile Pete and I are having more than usual difficulty in joining Bud under the bush as the ground underfoot is somewhat soggy. After slipping and sliding to and fro, we eventually manage to squat down into our usual but waterlogged places.

'I am so thrilled that you made it today as I want you to greet Forest,' Bud states with delight.

Pete and I look round and then glance at one another suspiciously as we can only count three of us present. The grin is still firmly fixed on Bud's face. Pete and I smile awkwardly in an attempt to humour him. An embarrassing moment occurs as he grins at us and we smile back at him.

Just as we think that Bud must have lost the plot a lingering 'he…. llo' wafts out from the shadows followed immediately by the owner. Accompanied by a rustling of leaves, the mini-tree one materialises from the darkness as if by magic.

'Oh! You scared us half to death,' gasp Pete and me.

'I can ashaw you'all that was not ma intention. Ah thought you realised that Ah was here,' drawls Forest in a strong southern American accent.

As if it made any difference whether we knew he was there or not who in their right mind would be shocked by the sudden arrival of a walking, talking stick with clumps of foliage shooting out from various points of its anatomy? I had thought that we were over being surprised by these little guys but I guess it will just take a while longer to become accustomed to the gang. A wry smile nudges Bud's face as he swiftly takes the matter in hand.

'Forest dropped in quite unexpectedly yesterday so I thought this would be a good opportunity for you to get to know him better,' Bud recommends, 'but he does not have much time to spare as he has a very urgent problem to attend to.'

Meanwhile Pete and I have just about got our wits together and feel the ability to speak returning to our lips. The last time we laid eyes on Forest, I made a pathetic joke about his name. I can only hope that he has got a short memory.

'Where have you come from?' I venture.

'Ah have popped in on ma way back from the Kibale Forest National Park in Western Uganda where the situation is most grave,' Forest draws out his words as he moves a little closer towards us, 'in fact, Wee Beastie is still there as we speak trying to calm down the situation.'

'I'm lost already,' admits Pete.

'Could you spare a few moments to enlighten us?' entreats Bud.

'Well you'all really should be fully infawmed of recent developments,' a serious note to his voice almost shroud's Forest's southern accent, 'after decades of witnessing their habitat being hacked away and replaced by fawmland, the chimpanzees of the forest are taking revenge on humans. In the past 7 years, they have attacked 15 children in Western Uganda alone. Another spate has occurred in neighbouring Tanzania; the most recent being a 60 year old security guard who had his aihyes gouged out by a chimp while strolling alawng the beach.'

'Are you suggesting that these chimps are taking cold, calculated vengeance against humans?' The disbelief is very prominent in Pete's voice.

'For shaw,' insists Forest, 'Ah have it on complete awthority. Ah heard it straight from the hawse's mouth, you maight say. Wee Beastie who is responsible for the Animal Kingdom ashawed me that this resentment is not new because the chimps are tired of being bothered and pushed from place to place. When they faind that their usuawl places to find sugar caine or fruit have been cut down, then they go away and get angry. As great swathes of the forest have been turned over to tea plantations and villages, the chimps' traditional food supplies have been squeezed out.'

'I had no idea that chimpanzees attacked people. Aren't they afraid?' I wonder.

'A male chimp does not fear a woman or a chaild but will only challenge a full grown man if threatened,' Forest relays to us, 'but Ah can tell you that Wee Beastie has had his work cut out this taime. Although he has encouraged the chimps to be aggressive, he tried to warn them against being so violent that they maight get themselves killed. At the same taime, he wants them to highlight their cause but try to preserve their dwindling numbers. Do you'all know that over the past century, the world population of primates who are man's closest biological relative has been reduced by 90% from two and a hawlf million to just 250,000. Do you'all have any ahdea that 10% of this planet's 608 primate species are now in dainger of extainction? Are you awaire that in Indonesia alone every year an area of fawrest the saize of Switzerland disappears? At this rate, we estimate by the end of the next decaide, there will no fawrest left in Indonesia and the orang-utan native only to Borneo and Sumatra will be extinct in the wild.'

Forest has to stop to take a daip braith; he's got me at it naiw.

We soon learn that you can't keep a good twig down and before long he's up and at it again.

Without stopping to draw another gasp he *sticks* at it, 'baiby oraing-utains, their name means *man of the forest* in Indonesian, are sold as pets but when full-grown they become aggraissive which combained with fearsome straingth means that most are killed or abaindoned as soon as they reach adawlthood. In the not too distant future these orainge-haired tree dwellers will become baialawgical curiowsities faind only in zoos, private collections or in chimp sanctuaries.'

We can't fail to notice and be struck by the enthusiasm and dedication of all these little guys to their chosen subjects. On this occasion, Forest has obviously used a tad too much zeal for this speech as he looks visibly moved and slowly starts to wilt. Bud immediately senses Forest's predicament and asks one of us to lend a hand as the task is just a little too big for him to manage unaided.

I, the brave hero, volunteer and motion Pete to remain still for fear that if the two of us offer assistance we might end up squashing either Forest or Bud or worse still both of them. It is no simple

151

matter endeavouring to manoeuvre about a tiny limp tree supported on the one side by an overgrown bulb and by me in blind obedience on the other within the enclosed confines of a bush. Obviously unable to sit, Forest is eventually successfully propped up against a suitably strong branch. Here he is perfectly camouflaged; in fact it's a bit difficult to see where one begins and the other one ends. After a very brief but awkward respite as we have absolutely no idea what to say or do, thankfully Forest indicates by waggling about a few of his leaves that he is ready to resume.

He rises up refreshed and continues as if nothing has happened in the meantime, 'chimpanzees shaire 98.6% of human gaines so they feel the saime emotions as humans. They laugh if you tickle thaim; they will craiy if they are unhaippy. The femailes display the saime maternal instincts as a human mother. In Africa when hunters draig the babies off their dead mothers, you can see the obvious grief on those babies' faices. The agony they endure is no different to what a human would suffer,' he starts to wobble again.

Bud looks naturally worried as he leans forward to lend another shoot for support but Forest puts up a leaf as a sign that all is well.

'Hunters have even repawted that when looking down the barrel of a gun, the ape often adawpts a pleading expression and holds out its hand to the killers. Tragically the bushmeat hunters taike no notice at awll,' Forest sighs.

'That's sick,' I use the brief pause to add my comments on the subject and can see from Pete's nodding head that he agrees.

Before emotion has time to take hold of him again, Forest rallies round with this warning, 'your scientists have at laist discovered a retrovirus which is the saime faimily as HIV in a number of the hunters. The bushmeat is a most laikely sawrce of HIV infection in the human population. Do you'all realise that the deadly Ebola virus not only kills up to 80% of all humans it infects but can also survaive even in an animal cawpse?'

Before we have the chance to reveal our ignorance or throw up at the thought of diseased dead animals, this grand announcement by Forest seems to knock him sideways again so in order to avoid any more twig shuffling antics, Bud politely requests us to try to seek out some nourishment for everyone. We are happy to oblige as we are also feeling peckish and in need of stretching our limbs.

'Crikey, it's lunch time already,' I mutter glancing at my wristwatch.

'Do you not know instinctively when you require nourishment?' Bud looks astonished, 'it is a waste of resources to eat for the sake of eating,'

153

'We'll be as quick as possible,' we call as we clamber out from beneath the bush.

'Don't hurry yourselves,' Bud acknowledges, 'we'll be waiting here for your return.'

'What do twigs eat?' queries Pete with a shrug of his shoulders as we make our way towards the house.

'I haven't got a clue. I thought they only drank water but hey what do I know?' I reply, 'but our biggest problem will be trying to sneak out with whatever comes to hand if Wynken, Blynken and Nod have returned from their exploits on the pond. I hope they did not take all the bread to feed the birds.'

The house is quiet and empty for the time being so we set about raiding the fridge and the kitchen cupboards at breakneck speed. The bread bin is bare but we find two packets of prawn cocktail flavour crisps, half a packet of chocolate fingers and a lump of cheese. Not much of a selection but beggars can't be choosers. Before we can make a clean getaway, we hear the front door shut followed by the unmistakable footsteps of Double Trouble galloping down the hallway.

'Hello,' coos Charlie.

'What you doing?' Emily chimes in, 'Why have you got all that food? Can we come with you?'

'No!' is my abrupt reaction as we attempt to conceal the goodies about our persons.

Now Hitler plus dog join us. Her face expresses her great displeasure at my attitude towards the girls.

'And just why precisely can't they play out in the garden with you two?' she demands, 'it won't hurt you to amuse the girls for a while before they have to go home?'

'We got fed up sitting outside so we thought we would come in and watch a video,' I lie through my teeth.

'It's too nice now to stay inside. Find something to do in the garden. Now off you go,' Hitler has spoken.

Houston we have a real problem. We have a hungry plant and a twig in need of urgent resuscitation. We also have two soppy girls and a dog in need of urgent elimination. I grab hold of Spot afraid that he will make a beeline for the bush and give the game away. I gingerly open the French doors to delay our exit whilst I mentally and quickly devise a cunning plan.

Everything is under control until the order to get a move on is issued by Hitler. Then pandemonium breaks out as I am tugged from the front and shoved from the rear. I suddenly find myself outside quicker than intended. My hand is still wedged firmly to Spot's collar but he is doing his utmost to tear us apart. This causes great hilarity with the girls who stand on the patio giggling in anticipation of me being pulled headlong into the mud. I fear I cannot hold onto the struggling beast for much longer.

'What now?' I glare at Pete, 'can't you think of **something**?'

'Mrs Martin it's probably not a good idea if the two girls play out in the garden, it' s very muddy underfoot and mum didn't want them to spoil their new dresses.'

'Perhaps they should sit and watch a movie until it's time to go home,' agrees Hitler, 'I'll give you a call at 4.30 Peter and you can walk them back.'

Well done Pete. They don't call him the *Master of Invention* for nothing. Now there is only the small matter of the dog. Just as I'm about ready to admit defeat, luck strikes twice in one day. Hitler decides that the dog could do with a bath as he has been wallowing in the pond and has not come out smelling of roses! In the nick of time, Hitler throws the dog's towel over him and marshals the unwilling prisoner back into the kitchen. The colour coordinated duo obediently toddle off close behind as we strive to contain our very obvious sense of relief.

Once out of Hitler's sight Pete and I happily *high five*.

Danger averted once more; can't help feeling that Bud must be rooting for us. We amble towards the bush casually stopping to nibble a couple of crisps en route while we wait for the assembled gathering to disappear indoors. As soon as they are gone, we make a dash for the bush.

'That was quite a commotion. What was going on?' all the noise has aroused Bud's curiosity.

'It was my younger sister, Emily, and her friend who wanted to join us,' Pete lets them know, 'we only just managed to get away. I have to take them home at 4.30 so you will excuse us if we keep tabs on the time?'

We quickly retrieve all our offerings from our cramped pockets and just as quickly apologise for their squashed condition. Our words are lost on deaf ears as our famished flora wolf down every single crumb as if food is going out of fashion.

'We can't thank you enough,' Bud utters, 'we were certainly in need of refreshment. I have to say I am a bit partial to those chocolate sticks.'

'It's our pleasure,' we assure them, 'those sticks are called chocolate fingers, why we don't know as they bear no resemblance to fingers whatsoever. We hope they were OK with the prawn cocktail crisps but that was all we could find?'

'Whatever they are called, they are delicious.' They definitely did the trick as Forest is revitalised and ready to start afresh if you so wish,' Bud informs us.

157

'Yes, as soon as possible please as we have to keep an eye on the time.'

'There you go again with your clock watching,' Bud almost despairs of us, 'but in this instance, I appreciate your dilemma. Forest if you would be so kind.'

Forest detaches himself from his support a little too vigorously and begins to lurch forward. Pete spots the danger at once and stretches out his hand. With a gentle nudge from his index finger, Pete restores Forest to his upright position. Forest is visibly grateful but, being a trifle top heavy due to the seasonal deluge of greenery, refrains from taking a bow for obvious reasons. He hesitantly moves forward with branches flailing all over the place and takes a sharp intake of breath before rambling on with gusto.

'We had thawght that you had learned your laisson when Big M bestowed Dutch Elm disease upon you'all. In 1968 the British landscaipe was chainged faw ever as six and a half million elegant elm trees succumbed to this fungus.'

'You can say that again,' I interrupt the proceedings, 'we live on Elm Street and there isn't a single elm tree in sight.'

'Well you have first haind experience of the disawster,' acknowledges Forest, 'now, sadly, the glawrious Oak is in dainger.'

'Is this Big M's handiwork?' I venture to ask.

'Why, naturally,' responds Forest as if there were any doubt, 'Sudden Oak Death is the new plague from acraws the Atlaintic which threatens not just the oak but awll Britain's trees. But it is the oak tree that is quite literally rooted in yaw history. Perhaps the most famous one of awll is the Royal Oak at Boscobel near Telford in Shropshire where the future King Charles II hid while on the run from Cromwell and his awrmy following his defeat at the Battle of Worcester in 1651. Country folk say that an oak is: *Three hundred years a growing; 300 years a living; 300 hundred years a dying.*'

The very mention of death or dying and Forest's voice trembles with emotion causing him to sway once more. Fortunately on this occasion, only his ability to speak wavers but a few of his leaves do quiver slightly as his balance falters a little. He really is a delicate creature and in fairness to others perhaps should be labelled *handle with care*.

Needless to say, Pete and I remain on constant *red alert*; ready at a moment's notice to lend a helping hand or to be more precise a steadying finger. Too much eagerness from either one of us to assist the tumbling twiglet and we could find ourselves gathering up a bundle of firewood. This present wobble appears to be only a temporary setback as he quickly regains his composure to go on.

'Yaw constant awnslaught of uncontrollable logging not only destroys the haibitat of waildlife but also removes the trees which aict as barriers against natural hazards like mud slides and floods. Mankind is losing a veritable forest phawmacy of many as yet undiscovered medicinal plants. Tea tree oil has been used for medicinal pawrposes for centuries by Aborigines in Australia where the plant grows. The secret ingredient in tea tree oil you'all awlready use in some soaps, shampoos and antiseptic creams. By any chawnce, have you ever heard of echinacea?'

'No, where is it?' Pete is naturally inquisitive.

'Not so much *where* as *what*,' Forest puts an end to that conversation, 'echinacea grows as a wild flower on the American prairies and possesses antibiotic and antiviral properties which faight infection by increasing the qwuantity of whaite blood cells. It has long been used by the native Americans as a remedy for snake bites, infected wounds and saw throats.'

Forest now takes one of his almost compulsory breaks to get his breath back. Pete and I on stand by demonstrate our willingness to shuffle into action at a moment's notice but with a gentle smile and fleeting shake of his head Bud indicates that all is well again.

'Do you'all know that there are millions of sufferers worldwide of arthritis?' Forest is in full throttle once more, 'do you'all also know that there is an exotic fruit found in the South Sea Islands of the Pacific, the juice of which can offer pain relief to people suffering from arthritis?'

'Why is it so special?' It's my turn to sound like a bozo.

'Ahm glad you awsked that, 'Forest sounds pleased that his words are having some effect, 'the Noni fruit which is a member of the citrus family has anti-inflammatory chemicals and anti-bacterial compounds that work to block the cawses of pain. The fruit which is found in such places as Tahiti and Hawaii has been medicinally used for centuries by the inhabitants of the islands. There are so many maw that you need to find befaw taime runs out.'

He is sounding distressed so we stay at the ready.

'Ah am shaw that Ah have no need to tell you that malaria kills maw than 3,000 African children each day and a drug developed from the artemesia plant could provide one of the most powerful weapons against the spread of the deadly disease,' he musters every last bit of energy as he is keen to get his message across.

'We have the Eden Project which tries to teach people to live in harmony with nature without destroying it,' I'm amazed I said that.

161

'This is superb,' affirms Forest, 'we just hope that enough people will get the message before it is too late.'

'Sssshhh! Just a minute,' warns Pete. Alarm bells sound; everything comes to a grinding halt as Pete sits up, raises his hand and turns his head deliberately close to the opening in the bush to hear more clearly.

'Pete, Sam where are you?' the distinctive sound of Emily's voice trickles towards our hideout. Charlie's giggles disclose that Emily is not alone.

'Crikey, it's the Terrible Two; my sister and her annoying friend. You two had better skedaddle,' Pete whispers to our wary companions.

Without delay Bud and Forest are gone in the blink of an eye.

We, meanwhile, have to come up with some quick fire excuses to offset the barrage of questions that is about to rain down upon us.

'What you doing under that bush?' first Emily.
'Why aren't you coming out?' then Charlie.
'Why aren't you sitting out in the sun like mum said?' next Emily.
'Why can't you play out here with us?' followed again by Charlie.

'Why are you sitting all cramped under there?'
Emily's turn again.
'What have you got under there?' Charlie has
another go.

As we try to excavate ourselves out from under the
bush, we are simultaneously wracking our brains to
concoct some plausible answers.

'We are working on our school project which we
have to do over the summer,' Pete states
confidently.

'Why are you doing it under the bush?' the reply
does not appear to satisfy Emily's curiosity.

'We are studying the effects of photosynthesis on
leaves. We have to test the light energy absorbed by
chlorophyll,' Pete's response has completely floored
them.

It's knocked me sideways to tell the truth.

We have to discourage these two from delving any
deeper or we will have Hitler on our backs. At last,
they are bored with the subject of us and the bush.
They cheerfully suggest we take them to the
playground.

Pete, I am not worthy.

CHAPTER 12
Spyda's Web

Why is it you always get sick during the holidays? During term time you can stay home but who wants to take a *day off* in the holidays. Thank goodness, I haven't got the flu. Old Mrs Chambers at number 6 next door has been laid up for 4 days with the latest bout of obscure flu. She's is so old and wizened that normally she looks about 108, I dread to think what she looks like with full blown influenza.

Hitler keeps popping over there with buckets of home-made chicken broth. Why they call it broth is a mystery known only to the makers of broth; to anybody else it is soup. I am sure that chicken broth in the capable hands of a masterchef is most likely delicious; however Hitler's attempts defy description. You have to remember here that we are talking about my mother whose culinary skills are limited to ruining a takeaway. I cannot determine which of the two should be awarded the medal for bravery. There's Hitler advancing forth into the unknown armed only with vast quantities of soup, sorry broth; or there's Mrs C alone save only for her black cat, Tiddles, the same age in feline years as her mistress, having watery chicken gunk thrust upon her. I am not too sure whether this has helped or hindered the old lady's recovery but I am keeping a close lookout in case she starts sprouting feathers!

But I have enough problems of my own. So back to my predicament; I find myself cooped up in bed,

164

coughing and sneezing with a red nose to match Rudolph's to the tune of Hitler whining on about *that will teach me a lesson for sitting on the wet grass for so long.* I daren't even imply that she might have transported some of the migrant bugs back from the plague pit next door for fear that she might make me some of that soup!

It's no fun lounging in bed when you are supposed to be there. After one whole day of misery, I am quite understandably feeling bored. How come that when you're enjoying yourself you never have enough time to finish what you started? Yet when you're bored, time is endless? Boredom knows no bounds! If I get up to switch on the telly or get my IPod, Hitler only moans until my life becomes so unbearable that it's a relief to get back into bed. I call Pete and convince him that I am no longer contagious and in need of some stimulation. The good news is that he is coming over; the bad news is that he is bringing you know who and her soppy friend with him. There is no point in my coughing and sneezing all over them in the hope that it might discourage their stay because Pete is lumbered once again into looking after them. So it's either Pete plus twittering ensemble or not at all.

No choice then?

I am going to get dressed even if Hitler grumbles all day. I am not entertaining guests in my shrunken, Spiderman pyjamas. Even poor old Spiderman looks as if he is suffering. That would certainly be a cause for much hilarity with the daffy twosome, not that they need any excuse. I catch a glimpse in the mirror from where my ghostly reflection stares back at me. I appreciate that I must look grim, what I do not need is the mirror to confirm this. In my role as the *living dead,* I had better try to liven myself up before I crack the glass and have seven more years of bad luck to look forward to. So I put on my jeans and a blue hoodie to rejoin the land of the living. I am careful to avoid wearing anything white in case this prompts offers for me to haunt houses. I make my way downstairs conveniently to coincide with Pete & co's arrival at the front door. I get another warning from Hitler, this time about having to stay indoors. Still makes a change from being told to get some fresh air.

The gruesome girls have come laden with sparkly bags busting at the seams with lipsticks, nail polishes, hair clips and hair gel. Strangely, this fails to lift my black, self-sympathetic mood. In fact, thoughts of murder spring to mind; theirs not mine. I'm not feeling **that** depressed. Any hope of Hitler taking them off our hands quickly fades as she announces that she is going to inflict some more gruel on Mrs C and then get her hair cut. We now have the problem of occupying these two for at least a couple of hours. As I am confined to the house, a DVD would seem to be the obvious solution but we don't want to watch anything they like and any of ours would give them nightmares. As luck would have it, they disappear off somewhere with their goody bags to leave Pete and I in peace.

We become totally absorbed listening to Pete's iPod and lose all track of time. We are completely happy to leave matters as they are had not our contentment been ruined by the sound of toe-curling, ear-piercing screams resounding from the garden. This causes the dog's ears to prick up which is a shame as up to now he has been snoring peacefully in the corner. Another selection of high-pitched shrieks urges him to get up and start yelping by the French windows. The noise is so overwhelming that Pete and I force ourselves to investigate.

'What **is** wrong with those two idiots?' I ask more out of annoyance than in the hope that Pete might have the answer.

'I hope it's fatal,' Pete sounds as exasperated as I feel.

'I'll hold the dog while you deal with them,' I propose. I grab hold of Spot and try to winch him away from the door.

With the door just ajar, Pete tries the subtle approach, 'If you don't belt up I'll let the dog loose on you.'

This is to no avail.

More panic and pandemonium from the girls outside

More howling and fidgeting from the dog inside.

'If they have been stung or something, why don't they come in so that we can treat it?' I suggest.

'They are obviously not going to give us any peace so I'll have another listen out the door. Hold on to the dog will you,' requests Pete.

'Better still, I'll drag him into the kitchen out of the way.'

I am immediately beginning to regret having said this. I can hear Pete yelling at the girls from the lounge but I cannot decipher what they are replying as I am battling with the hound. With what little strength I am able to rally in my highly-pathetic state, I am yanking several pounds of reluctant dogmeat with the brakes firmly applied across the hallway. If his claws which are prone to being long scratch the newly-laid wood floor, Hitler will in turn mark me for life! I am sweating heavily; whether it is due to my cold or fear of the wrath of Hitler or to the tug of war with my dribbling friend is impossible to decide. I heave a heartfelt sigh of relief at mission accomplished as I shove man's best friend headfirst into the kitchen. Just as I am about to grab a well-earned drink to cool me down, I detect groaning sounds arising from the other room. I take this to mean that Pete is still having trouble with the painful pair.

'What's up?' I risk asking.

'They just won't stop making a fuss,' Pete cries out in desperation, obviously exhausted by all the wasted effort, 'I'll try once more.'

At which he opens the door to the garden and threatens at the top of his voice to personally throttle the girls if they do not shut up. They still carry on making their high-pitched row despite the imminent danger of *death by brother*. I join Pete in the lounge wondering what to do next in case the neighbours take it upon themselves to report a murder in process at number 8. Pete is hanging out the door by his left hand while his right hand is cupped behind his ear trying to make sense of the ranting and raving going on.

'If they would just stop screeching for five minutes, I could possibly hear what they are saying. They seem to be muttering something about …er… er… spider is all I can make out,' complains Pete shrugging his shoulders and looking decidedly nonplussed as he turns to face me.

'Oh! Is that all?' I must say I feel relieved, 'tell them to stamp on it or come inside till it's gone. Mind you with all the din that they are creating, it's probably miles away by now.'

'They say they are frightened that it might come after them besides they can't stamp on it because it's huge,' huffs Pete.

Pete and I stop dead in our tracks. We turn to face each other eyes and mouths wide open. For umpteen seconds we neither blink nor breathe. The brain cells kick in as the shock begins to fade.

'A huge spider! Oh no!' Pete and I gasp as reality dawns. We zoom out into the garden almost colliding in the charge. In the nick of time, I catch hold of his arm and urge him to slow down so as not give the girls any more cause for alarm. Pete agrees and we approach them cool, calm and collected.

We edge towards the two of them now huddled together too scared to move; rooted to the spot on one of the rare clumps of grass in the garden; their bright pink faces streamed from trickles of tears complete their matching ensembles.

'You saw a spider, yes?' confirms Pete quietly intent upon pacifying the girls.

They nod in terrified unison.

'Now where did you see this spider?' I softly ask.

'Un..un..under that bush,' sobs Emily.

'It was **enormous**,' snivels Charlie.

'You must be mistaken,' I suggest in my caring mode; anything to quieten the noisy perishers down, 'but I'll go and have a look anyway just to be sure.'

'We weren't mistaken. It was huge and it was under **that** bush,' stresses Emily as she points in no uncertain terms to our bush.

Our intrepid hero, that's me in case you did not instantly recognise the description, marches bravely towards the bush, inwardly praying that I only discover a pile of leaves when I eventually get there. I lean forward anxiously and cautiously peer underneath.

'Well, there's nothing there now,' I insist in a loud voice which I also hope might scare away anything which could be lurking. I cast a sly glance of relief at Pete.

'Come and see for yourselves if you won't take my word for it,' I confidently suggest secretly crossing my fingers behind my back in case they feel tempted to take up the offer. Meanwhile Pete stands ready to restrain the pair should curiosity get the better of them and overcome their fear.

'Well, it **was** when we looked under there,' Emily refuses to be budged. She has switched from trembly to stubborn mood.

'All that noise you two were making has scared it clean away. Or perhaps it was a trick of the light. It's quite dark under that bush. So you can relax now. Why don't you come inside and have a drink?' I offer.

This idea seems to appeal as they appear convinced by at least one of our explanations. So we coax them gently back indoors out of harm's way. We sit them down quietly and ply them with drinks and crisps, desperately trying to calm them down before Hitler returns to scenes of chaos.

We only have about five minutes wait before the dreaded happens; Hitler comes bounding in to witness us pouring sympathy over the girls.

'What have you done to these two?' she accuses us outright.

Guilty before proved innocent.

'We haven't done *anything,*' I protest.

'Then why have they been crying?' she persists, 'you must have done something to upset them? And why have you been outside when I strictly told you not to?'

'If you just hang on a minute, I'll tell you the reason,' I am adamant she is going to listen. It must be the flu or the thought of the homemade broth that has made me so bolshie. Anyway, it has the desired effect as she stops arms folded to await my satisfactory explanation.

'Well, I'm waiting?' forehead frowned, eyes squinted, lips pursed, teeth gritted, she throws down the gauntlet.

'The girls thought they saw a big spider in the garden so we went out to help them,' I put the case for the defence. Before I can continue my opening address to the court of Hitler, the nuisances rudely and deafeningly pipe in.

'We **did** see a spider,' yells Emily.
'And it wasn't **big** it was **huge**,' shrieks Charlie, 'I'm sure it was a tarantula.'

'Now girls we don't have tarantulas in this country,' Hitler is in teaching mode, 'if you were frightened of it why didn't you leave it alone and come indoors?'

'It kept staring and smiling at us. We thought it was going to chase us if we ran away,' bawls Emily.

'Will you please keep your voices down,' Hitler is becoming slightly irritated with the goings on, 'once and for all; spiders do not stare and most certainly do not smile. You can barely see their faces, they're so small.'

'We keep telling you **this** one was big,' the girls stand up and shout in tandem.

'I shan't tell you once more. Will you both please be quiet?' This time Hitler raises her voice but calms down to carry on, 'where exactly did you see this spider?'

'Under the bush at the end of the garden,' they wail in harmony.

'I will take you two down there to prove that it was just a trick of the light,' Hitler motions the girls outside.

'We already did that. I went and looked under the bush to show them it was all clear,' I exclaim rapidly and slightly in desperation.

'Now don't you start shouting,' Hitler issues the orders, 'if I don't put a stop to this nonsense once and for all, they will have nightmares.'

She ushers the nervous pair out into the garden and frogmarches them towards the bush; hotly pursued by us. We are dreading them finding any of the gang which would probably turn the girls even more psychotic than they already are and as for Hitler, she would most likely burn the bush to the ground. Hitler blunders in and retreats with assurances that there is absolutely nothing inside apart from leaves and branches. With a bit of friendly persuasion, the girls are edged under the foliage. They back out very quickly nodding in agreement that it is arachnid free. Drama over; we all retreat back to the house for refreshment before Pete thankfully drags them back home.

The next day, Hitler agrees I am fit enough to wander outside even though it rained all through the night. She believes my assurances that I will not go out if it starts raining again. She is going over to Pete's house to try and explain what happened to the girls yesterday which leaves Pete clear to come over here. Blissfully, the dopey duo have requested the presence of the dog so I always the helpful one attach the lead to his collar and bundle him out the front door. Pete's arrival coincides opportunely with Hitler's departure. After a couple of swift token *hellos and goodbyes*, we are left to our own devices.

The rain has cleared up quickly to leave a very hot sun emerging. Pete and I need no persuasion. I look at him; he looks at me. We speedily race up the garden but our pace slackens as we get nearer to the bush.

'What if there really is a dirty great spider in there?' I mention as we are within striking distance of our target.

'We've got to find out, haven't we?'

'Yeah, I know,' I agree hesitantly with my nerves of excitement and terror waging outright war in my stomach, 'do you want to go first or shall I?'

'I don't mind. What do you reckon?'

'Up to you, really.'

'You've been unwell. Are you sure you feel up to it?'

'I think we owe it to the girls to find out, don't you?'

'Well, we can't put it off for ever. Are we going in or aren't we?'

We have stalled for time long enough so we elect to bravely go together before we realise the stupidity of our decision as the aperture to the bush is barely large enough to allow access for one. Still we take a deep breath; pull ourselves together and barge in; only to back out even quicker recoiling in disbelief and gasping as one.

'Did you see what I thought I saw?' I blurt out. I am aware that I am staring blindly at Pete. It feels most weird.

'I dunno. What precisely do you think you saw?' babbles Pete, his stunned gaze fixed firmly on me.

'I'm not exactly sure,' confirms my uncertainty.

'You tell me what you think you saw and I'll tell you if it is the same as what I think I saw,' suggests Pete.

'You go first.'

'No, you go first.'

'OK I thought I saw a massive black spider grinning at me,' as soon as the words leave my lips, I doubt the credibility of them.

'That's what I believe I witnessed,' Pete confirms with the same look of sheer scepticism plastered all over his face.

'I think I am secretly hoping that it's not true,' I confess.

'Me too,' nods Pete in agreement becoming the second instant member of *The Coward's Society.*

'What do you suggest we do now?' I am seeking Pete's willingness to go back and have another look.

While we are both standing there dithering, trying to pluck up courage for a second onslaught, a small familiar voice drifts out from under the bush which we instantly recognise as that belonging to Bud, beseeching us to come back in. Pete and I cast a *well what do you reckon* glance at each other; I shrug my shoulders; he shrugs his shoulders and to the cries of *Geronimo* in we dive headfirst.

We almost fail to notice Bud's welcoming smile as we crouch transfixed at the sight of his companion. No wonder the two girls were terrified out of their wits. Albeit that their wits were minimal to start with, this is one scary spectacle. We are literally face to face with this giant black, very hairy arachnid with its legs splayed out all over the place looking to all intents and purposes like a bigger variety of one of those hairy blackcurrant sweets gran excavates from the depths of her handbag. Nearly squashed alongside this hairy beast, we just about notice Bud perched nonchalantly on a stone apparently reading a scrap of newspaper.

'Ssshh! Sit and be quiet,' Bud motions us to the only available spot under the bush, 'he likes to rest to conserve his energy.'

We quietly oblige as we are perfectly happy not to wake the slumbering giant.

'Are you aware that in the Jungles of the Amazon, the Communal Territorial Orb Spiders in order to conserve their energy, gather in their thousands to build one massive web capable of entangling their prey,' Bud cheerfully informs us.

'You don't say,' mutters Pete with his stare fixed firmly on our dozing companion.

'Did I see you reading a piece of newspaper as we entered?' I put forward half out of curiosity; half out of need to ease the situation.

'You did indeed but did I detect a note of doubt in your voice?'

'Well sort of. I wasn't sure that you could read,' I reply hesitantly, instantly wondering whether I had touched a raw nerve.

Pete for a second turns his stare towards me with one of those *I wish you hadn't said that* expressions on his face. I cast my eyes upwards and screw up my mouth trying to cover my embarrassment. Too late!!

'Now you have offended me,' sighs Bud, more sad than insulted.

'I am so sorry. I did not mean that to come out the way it did,' I struggle with my feeble attempt at an apology.

Bud swiftly pulls himself together, obviously deciding to forgive my faux pas; rises defiantly from his stone to the full height of his stem to adopt lecture mode. Mind you after a remark like mine, we probably do need a good talking to.

'Now let me fill you in as they say in the movies,' Bud announces,' there are over 6,500 languages and many different writing systems worldwide. At Ego Friendly Dot Org, we have the responsibility of not only preserving but also of communicating in all 195 countries, 7 continents, and 5 oceans that make up this planet.'

Pete and I are speechless. The look of astonishment adorning our faces rapidly turns to one of acute embarrassment which just as sharply switches back to the eye popping, jaw dropping fix of sheer terror as we catch a glimpse of two, black glasslike mounds glistening in the centre of the once dormant mass to our right. The monster is awake. Bud is satisfied that we have suffered enough for our ignorance as he nimbly assembles all his leaves together to diplomatically diffuse a rather thorny situation.

'Meet Spyda,' Bud's words ease the almost tangible tension.

This causes a slit to emerge immediately below the two glassy pools amidst the black fuzz which gradually erupts into a parting spreading from east due west on Spyda's body. This we pray can be interpreted to mean a smile. In acknowledgement, all Pete and I can best manage is a facial illustration somewhat akin to a stunned snarl. We abruptly assume a more pleasing demeanour not wishing in any way to offend our most honoured guest.

'H..h..hi p..pleased to make your acquaintance,' I stammer pathetically with not a great deal of sincerity behind the greeting.

'Deelighted to meet you both at long last. I've heard such good reports about you from Bud here,' Spyda booms back, the downdraught from which almost expels us from beneath the bush in one fell swoop. He extends out one of his spiny tentacles in our direction but we both pull back uncertain at this point in time whether we are ready to be such close friends.

'Will you step into my den said the spider to the guy. Ha! Ha! Ha!' Spyda guffaws obviously amused by his own witticism. We too are bowled over not so much by his sense of humour more by the whiff of his breath. It is a bit overpowering to put it mildly but then we have not had much warning about what to expect as we have never been up this close and intimate with a spider before. Can't think this experience will figure highly on the *Top 100 Things To Do* list. What is it with these guys and their dental hygiene or rather lack of it?

'Step right in; I don't bite,' this sends him off again into convulsions of laughter which makes us consider that perhaps he is not so terrifying after all. Pete and I settle in to take up temporary residence for the time being and give Spyda the benefit of the doubt. We compose our faces hoping against hope that our expressions do not betray the truth. Bud looks relieved and relaxes happy to give his companion centre stage, well the entire space really.

'We understand that you are responsible for your website? Is that correct?' Pete asks determined that his tone should not sound patronising just in case this creature is prone to sudden mood swings, 'you don't use monitors or computers, do you?'

'No need of them, Old Boy,' Spyda asserts, 'Nature has been communicating with each other long before you were around. We have the most sophisticated and efficient system that you can only dream of. Would you like to learn some of our little secrets?'

'Yeah!' we confirm together. Spyda appears pleased with our decision and settles back into a comfortable spidery position. This move not only makes us feel a little easier but has the added bonus of removing us out of breathing range.

'Everything in Nature is inextricably linked and exists within a giant network which we call the 'Web of Life,'' he booms energetically, 'the world is sustained by invisible fields whether it be gravitational or electromagnetic and I believe Bud tried to explain the mental fields to you?'

'You mean the fact that you possess mindvision?' checks Pete.

'The very same,' approves Spyda,' but in truth all our minds operate through mental fields which extend far beyond the limits of the brain. Anyway back to electromagnetic fields which are present everywhere in the environment but are invisible to the human eye. The earth's magnetic field causes a compass needle to orient in a north-south direction which is used by birds and fish to navigate. If a bird loses its way, it can reprogramme its course. A turtle's brain contains magnetite to navigate by magnetic fields and can store the route like a computer. Are you with me so far?'

'Yep, we're keeping pace,' we heartily agree, anything so long as he doesn't laugh again.

'Good, then I shall continue,' he beams.

Not that we have the slightest intention of trying to stop him.

He merrily keeps going, 'besides the natural sources of the electromagnetic field there are also ones that you generate, for example, you use X-rays to diagnose broken bones and you also use different types of high frequency radio waves to transmit information via TV or computer antenna or mobile phone stations. Are you aware, for example, that even butterflies use radar to navigate?' he asks directly.

'Can't say that I'd given the subject much thought to be honest,' I admit somewhat bemused by the topic, 'you've explained how we communicate but what method do you use?'

'Exactly what I have been telling you,' Spyda seems affronted, 'we navigate and communicate. Every creature has a dominant sense which they use for protection, seeking food, or communicating. Dolphins, for example, use a skilful combination of sonar and intelligence to achieve this. Crocodiles sense the vibration in the water to pick up any message. No problems?' he bothers to find out.

'No we're fine,' we genuinely reassure our host who begins to grow on you after a while.

Bud looks pleasantly at ease.

'Swarm Intelligence is the term given to techniques used by the behaviour of social insects. This swarm intelligence is a system in which countless insects interact with each other and with their environment. As ants are highly social insects this system works like a single intelligence. Got that?' he is interested to ask.

'Sort of,' we mumble; not too sure we haven't drifted into the realm of science fiction.

'Bats,' he wants us know, 'have the ability to determine the position, the distance and even identify an object by measuring the time taken for an echo to return from the object. Whales and dolphins also have this skill which is called echolocation. As they usually hunt in murky waters where visibility is poor, they use echolocation to seek out their prey and to communicate with one another which we call *sight by sound*. Some humans who are blind can tap their canes and by interpreting the sound waves can identify the location and even the size of an obstacle so that they are able to avoid it. Every creature in Nature's system has its own unique way of communicating. We can relay a message any where in the world in next to no time,' Spyda looks well pleased and still raring to go.

At this point, all the talking and movement in such a confined space has taken its toll on the oxygen available. I start to feel slightly warm. I look to Pete to back me up not wishing to make a lone protest. Fortunately Bud picks up on my predicament and offers some comfort.

'Do you want to have a break?' he kindly offers.

'I am feeling a bit dry,' I confess, 'do you not get thirsty?'

'I read somewhere that spiders are bloodsuckers. Is this true?' Nervously asks Pete.

'We most certainly are not,' Spyda fervently denies, 'when we trap our prey, we inject venom into it which paralyses it. The venom then turns the insides of the prey into liquid which we might drink then or we save it for later. However at this moment in time, I will be satisfied with a little rain water.'

We both find ourselves wishing that Pete hadn't asked that question as we now feel slightly sick.

So as usual, Bud takes up our cause, 'luckily we plants rely upon a fungal system which supplies water to our roots and extracts sugar in return but why don't you get yourselves something to drink?' he wisely proposes.

'Is that OK with you?'

'Absolutely you have been very good and patient listeners. Off you go, we'll see you in a while,' smiles Bud as he waves us on our way. Spyda too nods in agreement.

So Pete and I do our best to remove ourselves from under the bush without thumping our gracious hosts in the process. We both amble towards the house endeavouring to straighten our spines into an upright position as we go but not one single word passes between us. Neither of us can get our heads round the fact that we have just been given a scientific lecture by an enormous articulate tarantula. There is no way we could even contemplate disclosing these events to anyone even if we wanted to. We can barely believe it and we sat through it.

'Do you think we should try to log on to their website just to see what happens?' the thought occurs to me as I break the silence.

'I have to admit I'm very tempted,' confesses Pete with a mischievous glint in his eye.

'Shall we go indoors and have a go,' I taunt us both.

Our reflection is irritatingly short lived as we are greeted at the door by Hitler demanding to know where we have been all afternoon.

'Your mother has been calling you Pete. She was complaining that your mobile was switched off,' Hitler sounds off at Pete.

'Sorry Mrs Martin, my battery is flat,' Pete squirms.

'Oh well never mind. You had better get home as soon as possible, if not sooner.'

'We were hoping to grab a drink and go back outside,' I give my doe eyed speciality impersonation of Spot to generate compassion for my appeal. This has no affect whatsoever with Mein Fuhrer.

'Not today, you're not. Perhaps tomorrow if nothing else is happening. Say goodbye to Pete and get ready for supper.'

Hitler has spoken. So we do not have the chance of going back to thank Bud and Spyda. They will probably think that we are so rude but we will apologise as soon as we see them again.

The trouble is we haven't seen them now for ages. Pete and I keep looking at every opportunity. I reckon they must have gone *underground.* Don't groan; I think it's rather clever. If Shakespeare makes a pun, we spend the next 400 years analysing its merits; if I use a similarly clever figure of speech everybody throws up! Just to prove to you that this touch of genius is not a fluke, I shall end with a poem.

For quite some time the Micro Guys have failed to show.
Rest assured if they do, you will be the first to know.

BIBLIOGRAPHY AND ACKNOWLEDGEMENTS

About.com. Washington DC

Associated Newspapers

BBC Archaeology in Depth

Cambridge Encyclopaedia. Cambridge. 1990

Chronicle of the World. Longman. 1989

Crocodilian Biology Database. 2004

Insecta Inspecta World. 2004

Lewis Carroll. Through the Looking Glass

Natural History Museum. Natural World

Natural History Museum. Palaeontology Department.

Wikipedia – on line encyclopaedia

Shelby Lin Erdman. Scientists reaffirm theory that giant asteroid killed dinosaurs March 08, 2010.CNN

Denver Eugene Field. "Wynken, Blynken, and Nod". Published 1889.

Rupert Sheldrake. The Sense of Being Stared At: and other aspects of the extended mind, New York, NY: Crown Publishers, 2003

Michael Hanlon. Science Editor. Daily Mail. 2010

Rupert Sheldrake. A New Science of Life: the hypothesis of formative causation, Los Angeles, CA: J.P. Tarcher, 1981

Nature Magazine. The discovery of the Antarctic "ozone hole" by British Antarctic Survey scientists Farman, Gardiner and Shanklin 1985

Sabrosky, C. W. 1952 Insects: The Yearbook of Agriculture. U.S. Dept. of Agr., Washington, D. C.

Internet Encyclopaedia of Philosophy. 2010

Laërtius & Hicks. V1 63, Plutarch, Moralia, 717c.Diogenes. 1925

www.bbc.co.uk Science & Nature. 2010

Charles Alexander Eastman. Living in Two Worlds: The American Indian Experience. Amazon

www.fossilmuseum.net. 2010

Rick Gore, Dinosaurs, National Geographic, pp. 42, Jan., 1993.

ScienceDaily (Aug. 18, 2010) —Decline of Mammals Durham University scientists

World Health Organisation Electromagnetic Fields

NASA Education Website. 2010

Dave Nalle. Argentine Ants Article. 2010

www.italymag.co.uk. 2010

ABC News / Health Channel. 2010

Mary Howitt. The Spider and the Fly

UK BBC NEWS. Ant supercolony dominates Europe. Tuesday, 16 April, 2002

T.H. Sissons. All of Time Online. 2004-2006

Made in the USA
San Bernardino, CA
30 March 2017